ZORRO®

™

PAPERCUTZ™

ZORRO®

Graphic Novels
Available from Papercutz

1 Scars!
2 Drownings! (Coming December 2005)
3 Vultures! (Coming March 2006)

$7.95 each in paperback
$12.95 each in hardcover

ALL-NEW, FULL-COLOR GRAPHIC NOVEL
ZORRO
#1
SCARS!
DON McGREGOR • SIDNEY LIMA
PAPERCUTZ

ZORRO
#2
PAPERCUTZ

ALL-NEW, FULL-COLOR GRAPHIC NOVEL
ZORRO
#3
PAPERCUTZ

Please add $3.00 for postage and handling for the first book, add $1.00 for each additional book.
Send for our catalog:
Papercutz
555 Eighth Avenue, Suite 1202
New York, NY 10018
www.papercutz.com

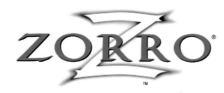

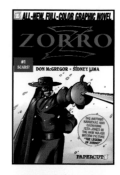

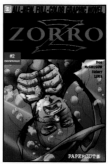

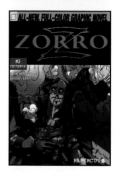

DON McGREGOR • Writer
SIDNEY LIMA • Artist
Based on the character created by
JOHNSTON McCULLEY

New York

This is for my wife, MARSHA CHILDERS McGREGOR – 27 years from our first night and the image of her moving with grace and beauty is a flesh and blood song in the heart and mind and soul, making fantasy and love real. – D.M.

Scars!
DON McGREGOR — Writer
SIDNEY LIMA — Artist
MARK LERER — Letterer
MARCOS de MIRANDA — Colorist
JIM SALICRUP — Editor-In-Chief

Special thanks to John Gertz and Sandra Curtis

ISBN 10: 1-59707-016-5 paperback edition
ISBN 13: 978-1-59707-016-4 paperback edition
ISBN 10: 1-59707-017-3 hardcover edition
ISBN 13: 978-1-59707-017-1 hardcover edition

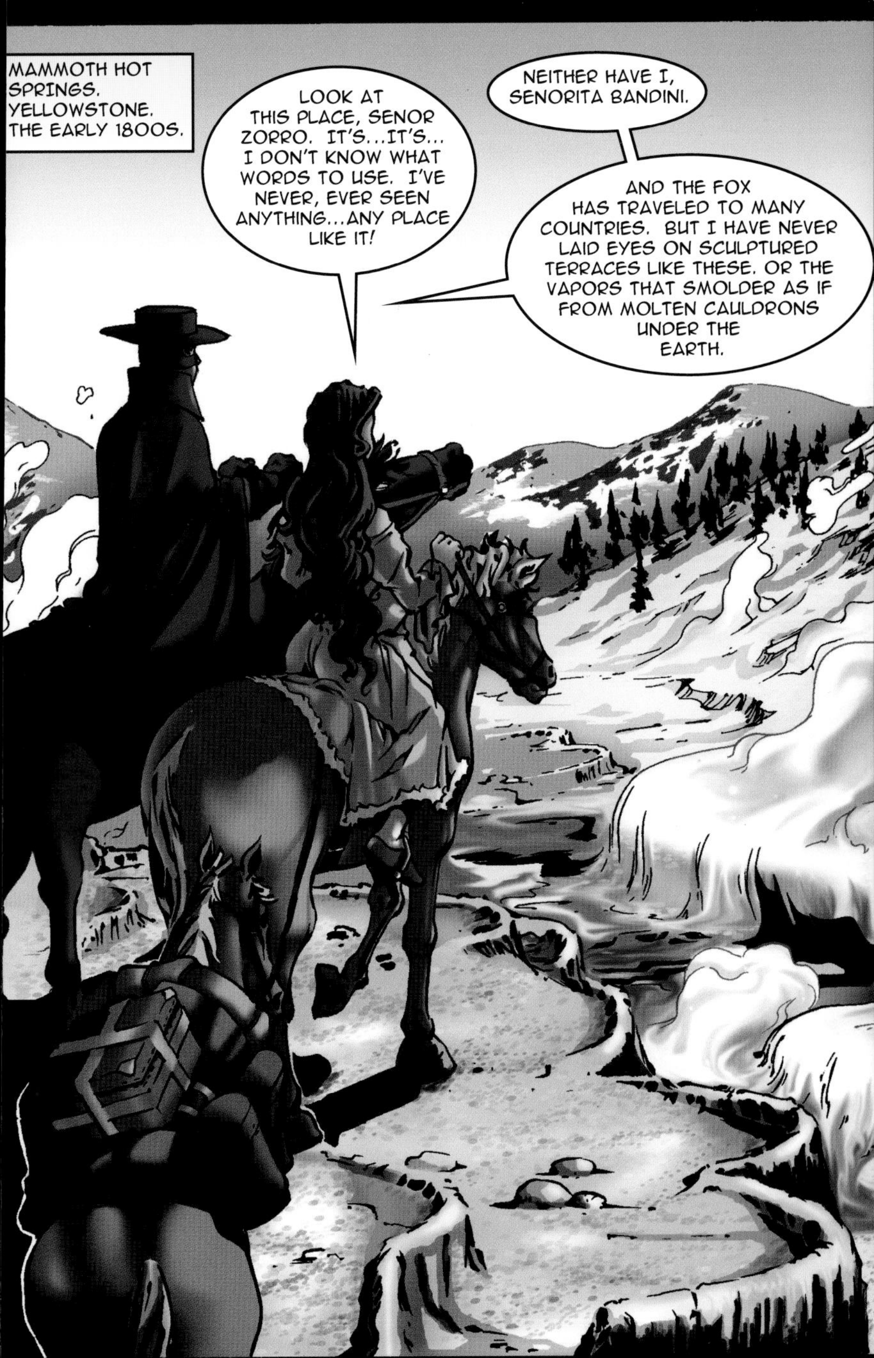
MAMMOTH HOT SPRINGS. YELLOWSTONE. THE EARLY 1800S.
LOOK AT THIS PLACE, SENOR ZORRO. IT'S...IT'S... I DON'T KNOW WHAT WORDS TO USE. I'VE NEVER, EVER SEEN ANYTHING...ANY PLACE LIKE IT!
NEITHER HAVE I, SENORITA BANDINI.
AND THE FOX HAS TRAVELED TO MANY COUNTRIES. BUT I HAVE NEVER LAID EYES ON SCULPTURED TERRACES LIKE THESE. OR THE VAPORS THAT SMOLDER AS IF FROM MOLTEN CAULDRONS UNDER THE EARTH.

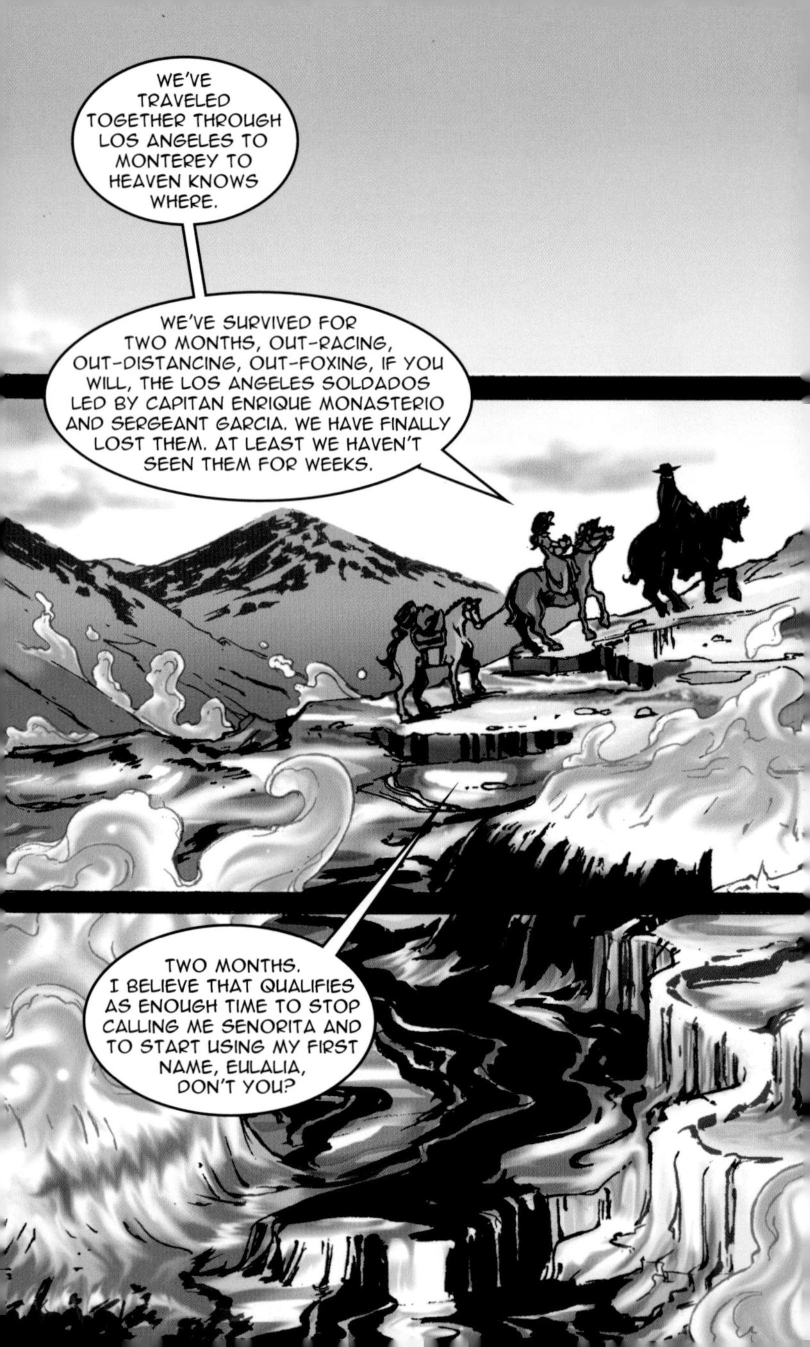
WE'VE TRAVELED TOGETHER THROUGH LOS ANGELES TO MONTEREY TO HEAVEN KNOWS WHERE.
WE'VE SURVIVED FOR TWO MONTHS, OUT-RACING, OUT-DISTANCING, OUT-FOXING, IF YOU WILL, THE LOS ANGELES SOLDADOS LED BY CAPITAN ENRIQUE MONASTERIO AND SERGEANT GARCIA. WE HAVE FINALLY LOST THEM. AT LEAST WE HAVEN'T SEEN THEM FOR WEEKS.
TWO MONTHS. I BELIEVE THAT QUALIFIES AS ENOUGH TIME TO STOP CALLING ME SENORITA AND TO START USING MY FIRST NAME, EULALIA, DON'T YOU?

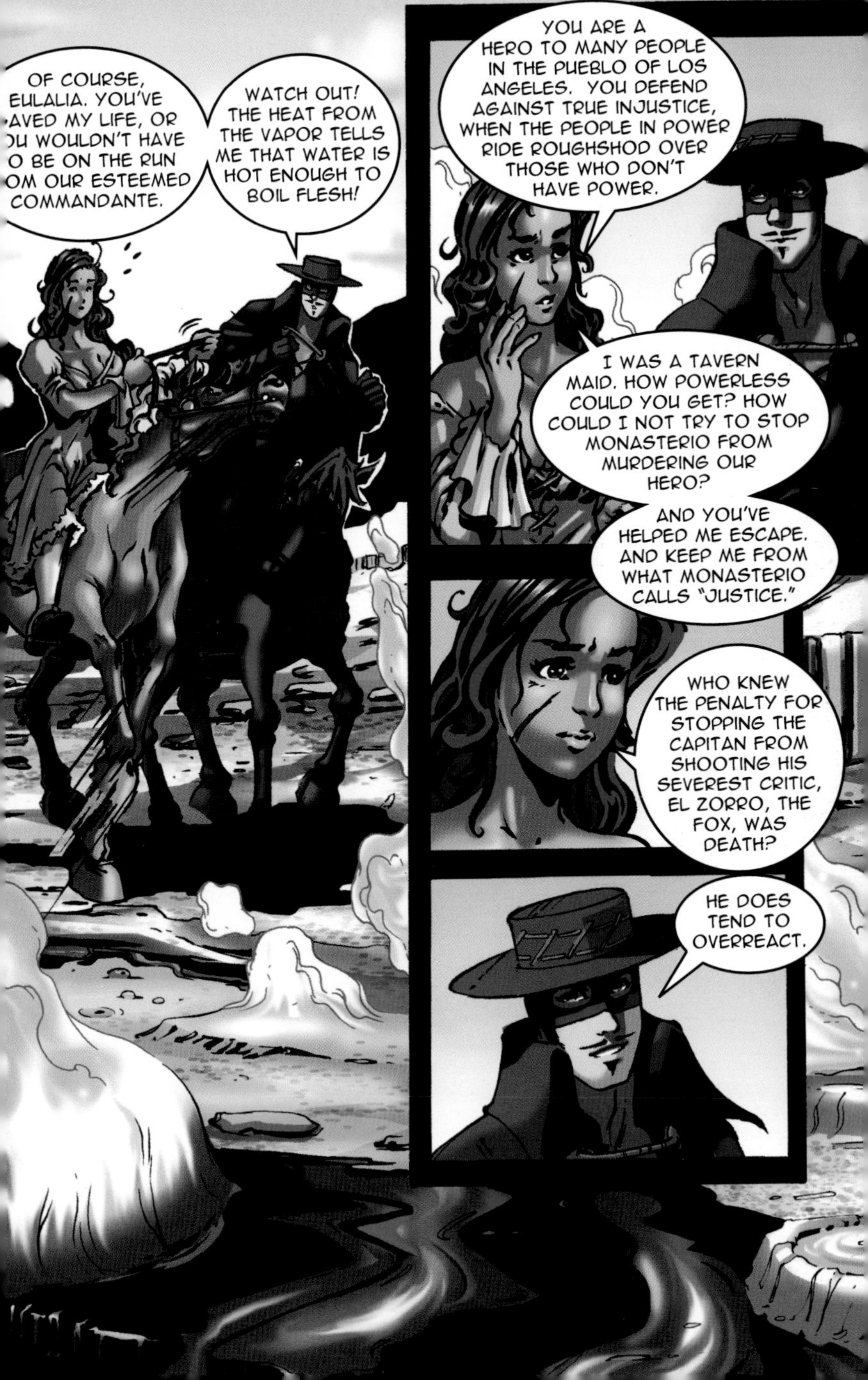

OF COURSE, EULALIA. YOU'VE AVED MY LIFE, OR OU WOULDN'T HAVE O BE ON THE RUN OM OUR ESTEEMED COMMANDANTE.
WATCH OUT! THE HEAT FROM THE VAPOR TELLS ME THAT WATER IS HOT ENOUGH TO BOIL FLESH!
YOU ARE A HERO TO MANY PEOPLE IN THE PUEBLO OF LOS ANGELES. YOU DEFEND AGAINST TRUE INJUSTICE, WHEN THE PEOPLE IN POWER RIDE ROUGHSHOD OVER THOSE WHO DON'T HAVE POWER.
I WAS A TAVERN MAID. HOW POWERLESS COULD YOU GET? HOW COULD I NOT TRY TO STOP MONASTERIO FROM MURDERING OUR HERO?
AND YOU'VE HELPED ME ESCAPE. AND KEEP ME FROM WHAT MONASTERIO CALLS "JUSTICE."
WHO KNEW THE PENALTY FOR STOPPING THE CAPITAN FROM SHOOTING HIS SEVEREST CRITIC, EL ZORRO, THE FOX, WAS DEATH?
HE DOES TEND TO OVERREACT.

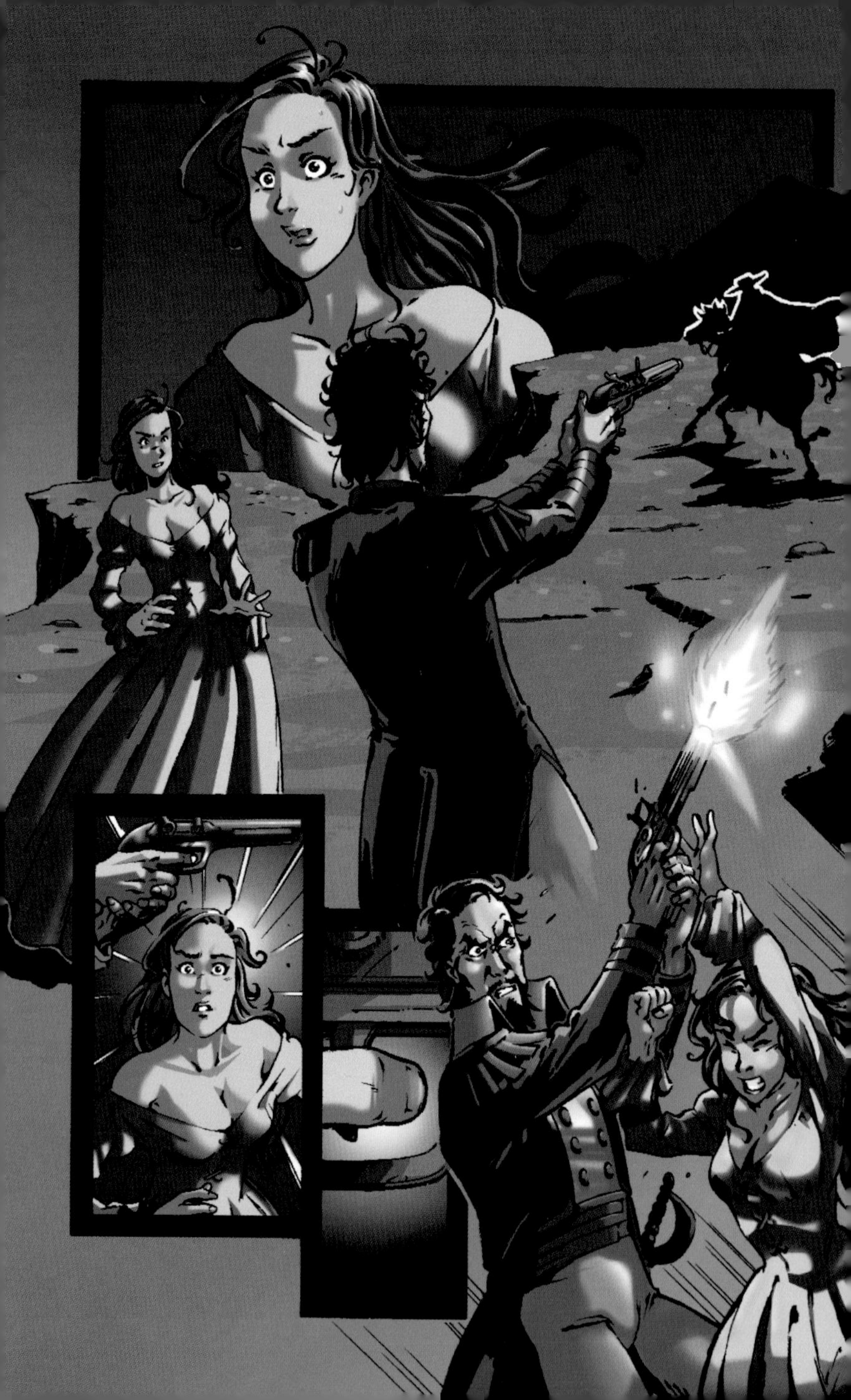

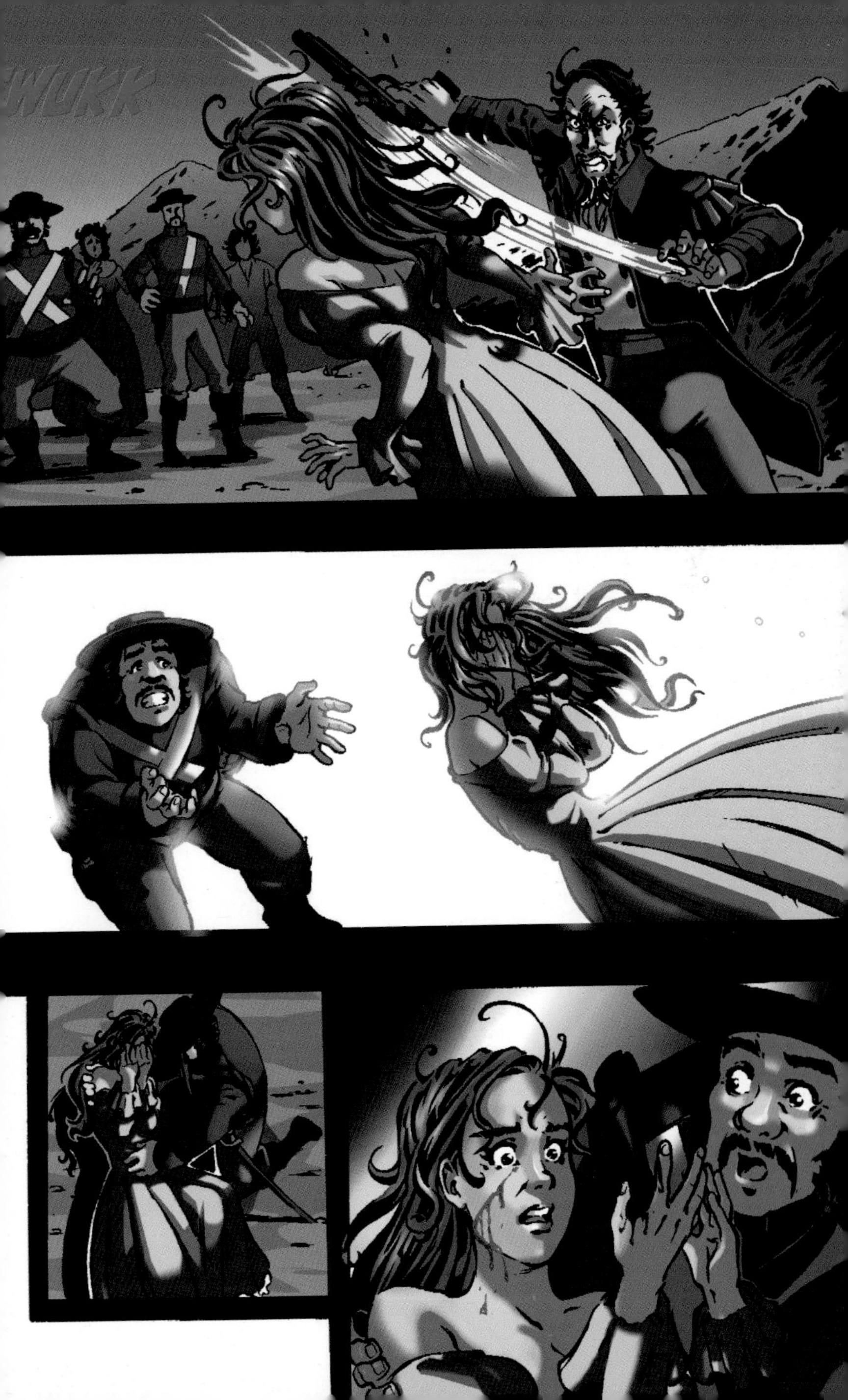
WUKK

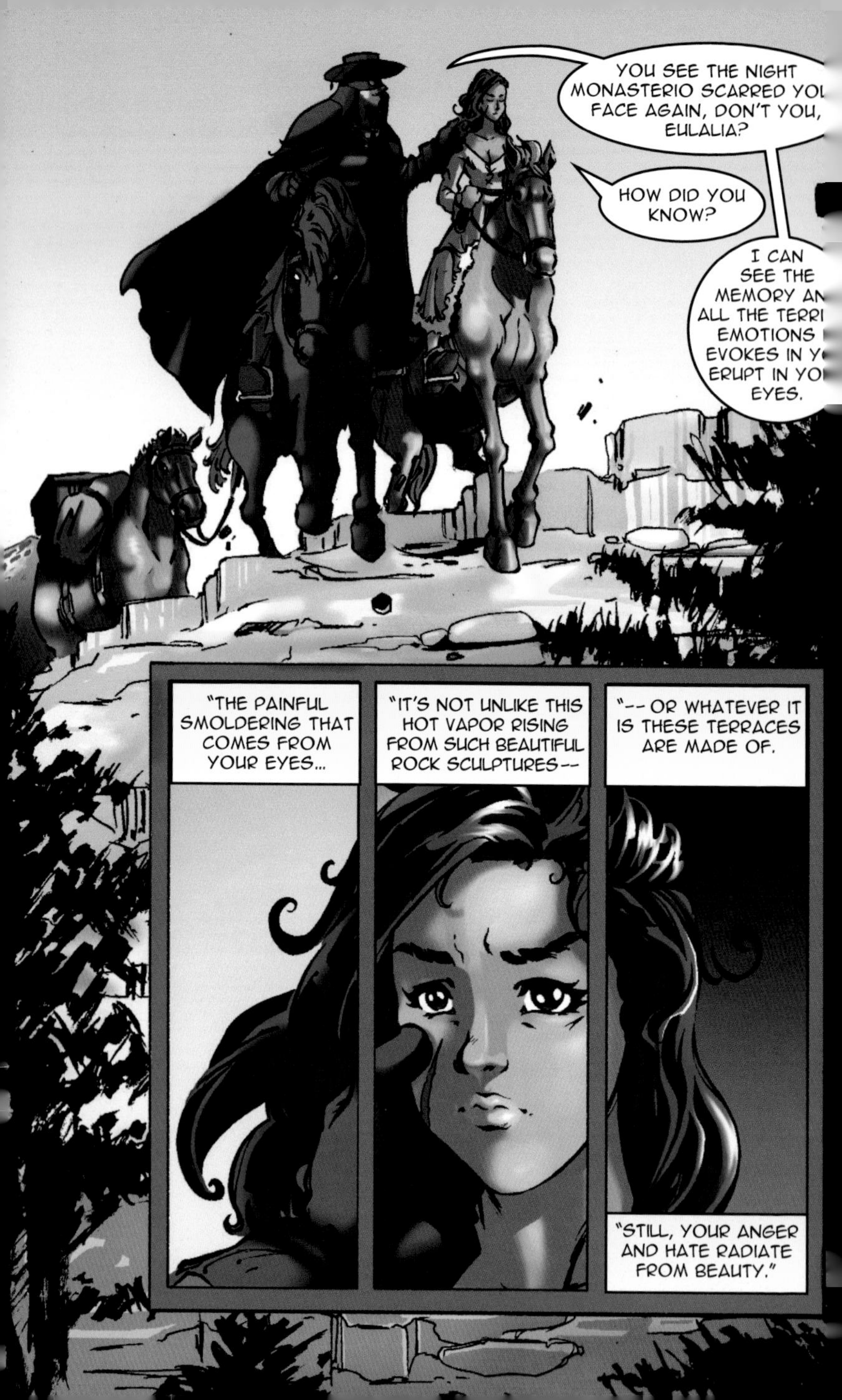
YOU SEE THE NIGHT MONASTERIO SCARRED YOU FACE AGAIN, DON'T YOU, EULALIA?
HOW DID YOU KNOW?
I CAN SEE THE MEMORY AN ALL THE TERRI EMOTIONS EVOKES IN Y ERUPT IN YO EYES.
"THE PAINFUL SMOLDERING THAT COMES FROM YOUR EYES...
"IT'S NOT UNLIKE THIS HOT VAPOR RISING FROM SUCH BEAUTIFUL ROCK SCULPTURES--
"-- OR WHATEVER IT IS THESE TERRACES ARE MADE OF.
"STILL, YOUR ANGER AND HATE RADIATE FROM BEAUTY."

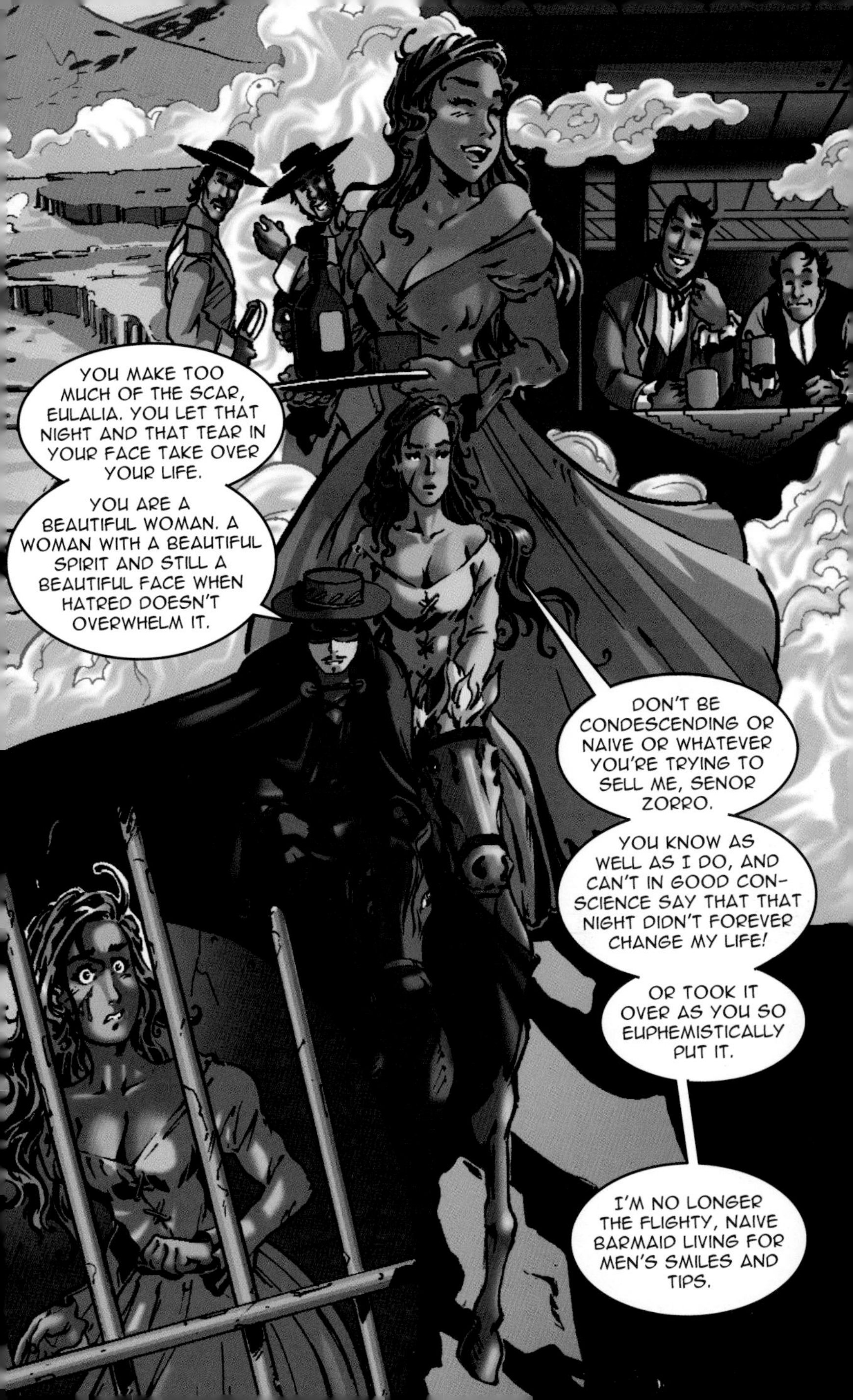
YOU MAKE TOO MUCH OF THE SCAR, EULALIA. YOU LET THAT NIGHT AND THAT TEAR IN YOUR FACE TAKE OVER YOUR LIFE.
YOU ARE A BEAUTIFUL WOMAN. A WOMAN WITH A BEAUTIFUL SPIRIT AND STILL A BEAUTIFUL FACE WHEN HATRED DOESN'T OVERWHELM IT.
DON'T BE CONDESCENDING OR NAIVE OR WHATEVER YOU'RE TRYING TO SELL ME, SENOR ZORRO.
YOU KNOW AS WELL AS I DO, AND CAN'T IN GOOD CON-SCIENCE SAY THAT THAT NIGHT DIDN'T FOREVER CHANGE MY LIFE!
OR TOOK IT OVER AS YOU SO EUPHEMISTICALLY PUT IT.
I'M NO LONGER THE FLIGHTY, NAIVE BARMAID LIVING FOR MEN'S SMILES AND TIPS.

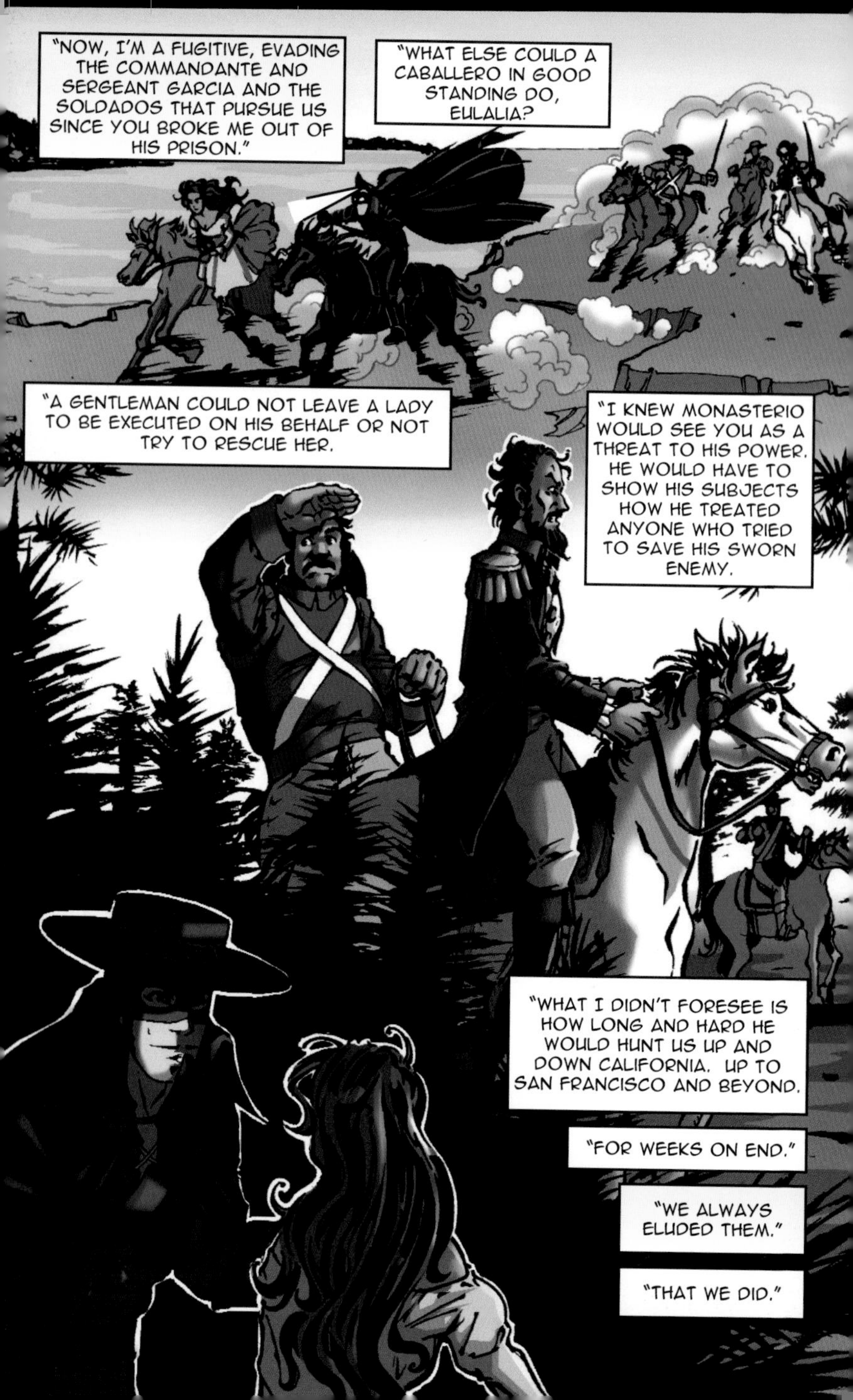
"NOW, I'M A FUGITIVE, EVADING THE COMMANDANTE AND SERGEANT GARCIA AND THE SOLDADOS THAT PURSUE US SINCE YOU BROKE ME OUT OF HIS PRISON."
"WHAT ELSE COULD A CABALLERO IN GOOD STANDING DO, EULALIA?
"A GENTLEMAN COULD NOT LEAVE A LADY TO BE EXECUTED ON HIS BEHALF OR NOT TRY TO RESCUE HER.
"I KNEW MONASTERIO WOULD SEE YOU AS A THREAT TO HIS POWER. HE WOULD HAVE TO SHOW HIS SUBJECTS HOW HE TREATED ANYONE WHO TRIED TO SAVE HIS SWORN ENEMY.
"WHAT I DIDN'T FORESEE IS HOW LONG AND HARD HE WOULD HUNT US UP AND DOWN CALIFORNIA. UP TO SAN FRANCISCO AND BEYOND.
"FOR WEEKS ON END."
"WE ALWAYS ELUDED THEM."
"THAT WE DID."

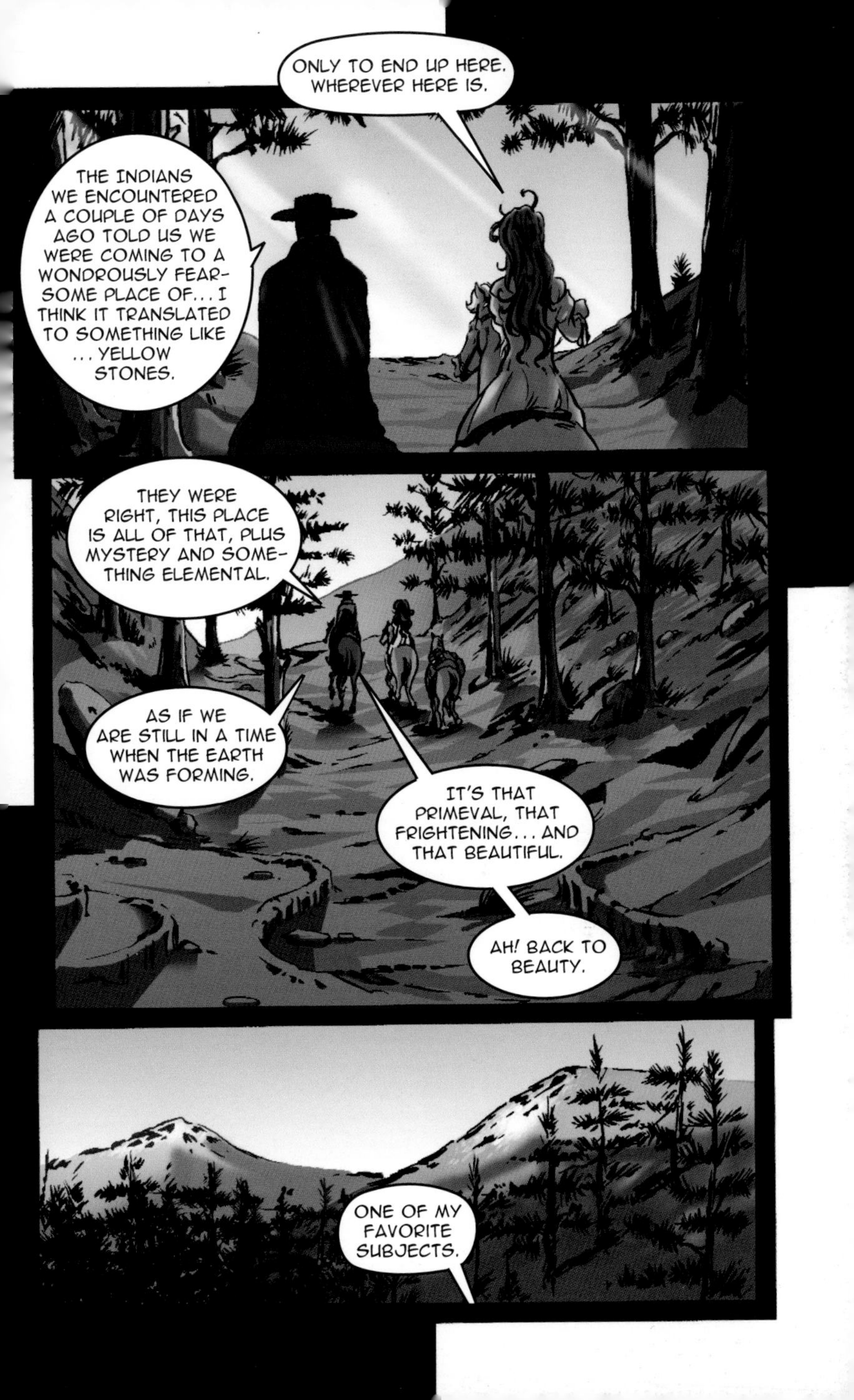
ONLY TO END UP HERE. WHEREVER HERE IS.
THE INDIANS WE ENCOUNTERED A COUPLE OF DAYS AGO TOLD US WE WERE COMING TO A WONDROUSLY FEAR-SOME PLACE OF... I THINK IT TRANSLATED TO SOMETHING LIKE ...YELLOW STONES.
THEY WERE RIGHT, THIS PLACE IS ALL OF THAT, PLUS MYSTERY AND SOME-THING ELEMENTAL.
AS IF WE ARE STILL IN A TIME WHEN THE EARTH WAS FORMING.
IT'S THAT PRIMEVAL, THAT FRIGHTENING... AND THAT BEAUTIFUL.
AH! BACK TO BEAUTY.
ONE OF MY FAVORITE SUBJECTS.

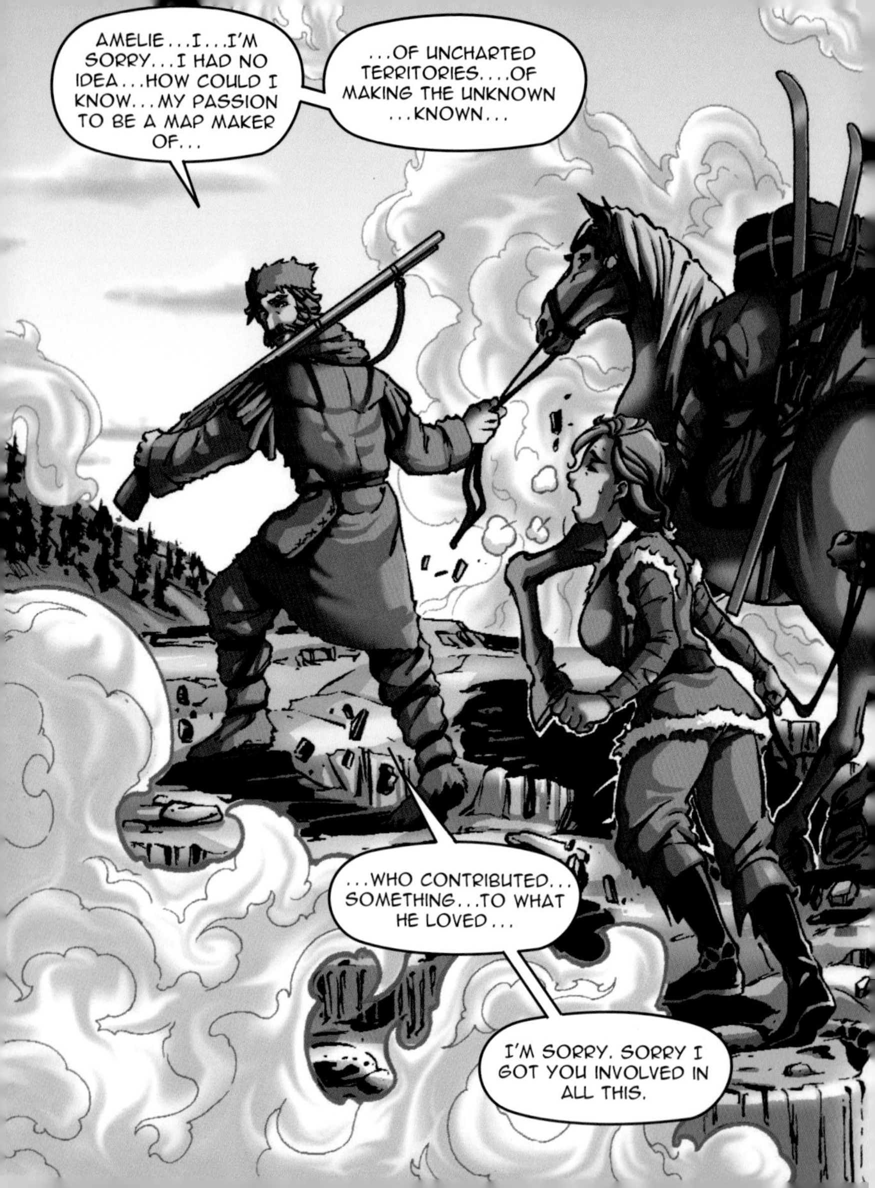
AMELIE...I...I'M SORRY...I HAD NO IDEA...HOW COULD I KNOW...MY PASSION TO BE A MAP MAKER OF...
...OF UNCHARTED TERRITORIES....OF MAKING THE UNKNOWN ...KNOWN...
...WHO CONTRIBUTED... SOMETHING...TO WHAT HE LOVED...
I'M SORRY. SORRY I GOT YOU INVOLVED IN ALL THIS.

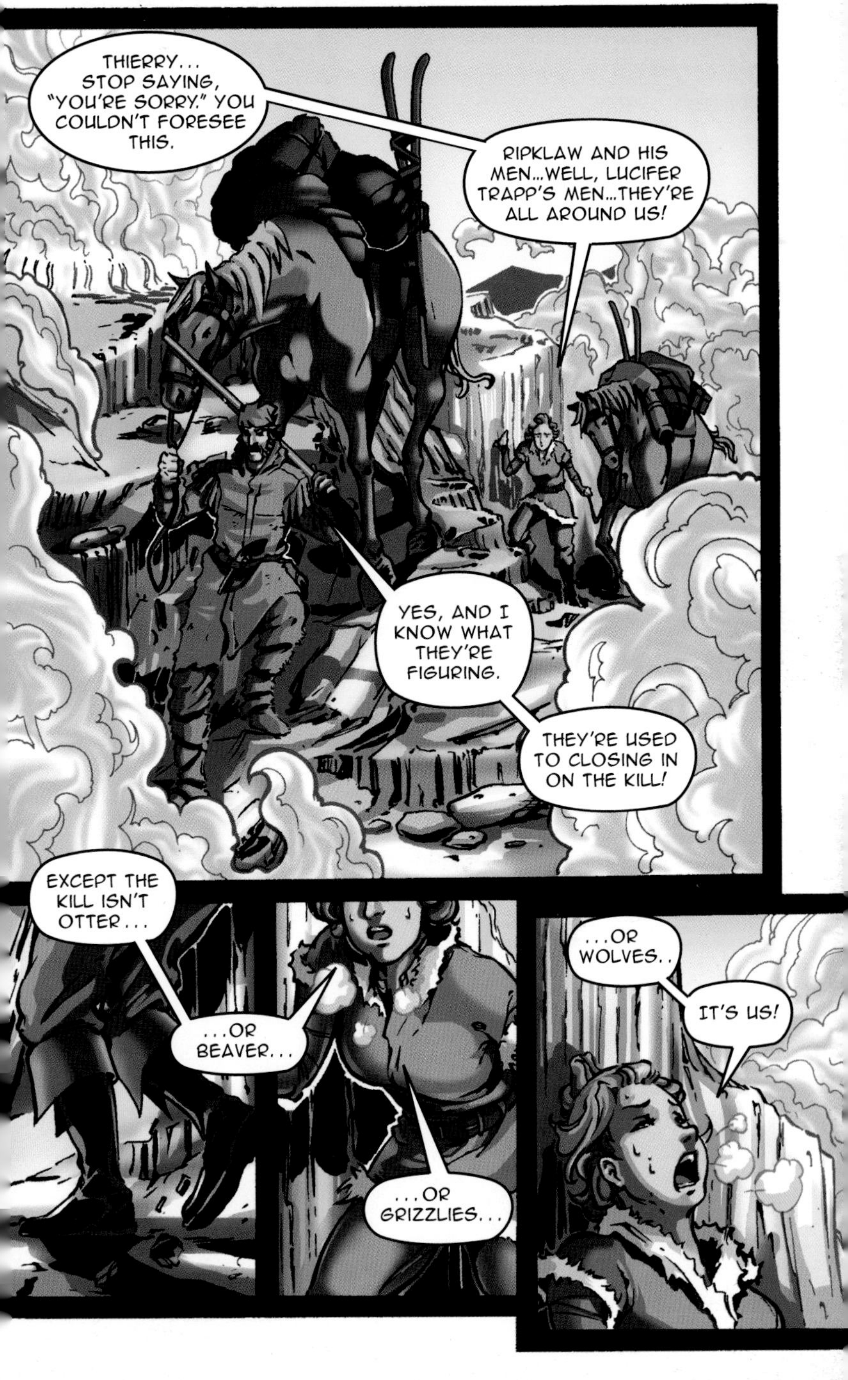
THIERRY... STOP SAYING, "YOU'RE SORRY." YOU COULDN'T FORESEE THIS.
RIPKLAW AND HIS MEN...WELL, LUCIFER TRAPP'S MEN...THEY'RE ALL AROUND US!
YES, AND I KNOW WHAT THEY'RE FIGURING.
THEY'RE USED TO CLOSING IN ON THE KILL!
EXCEPT THE KILL ISN'T OTTER...
...OR BEAVER...
...OR GRIZZLIES...
...OR WOLVES..
IT'S US!

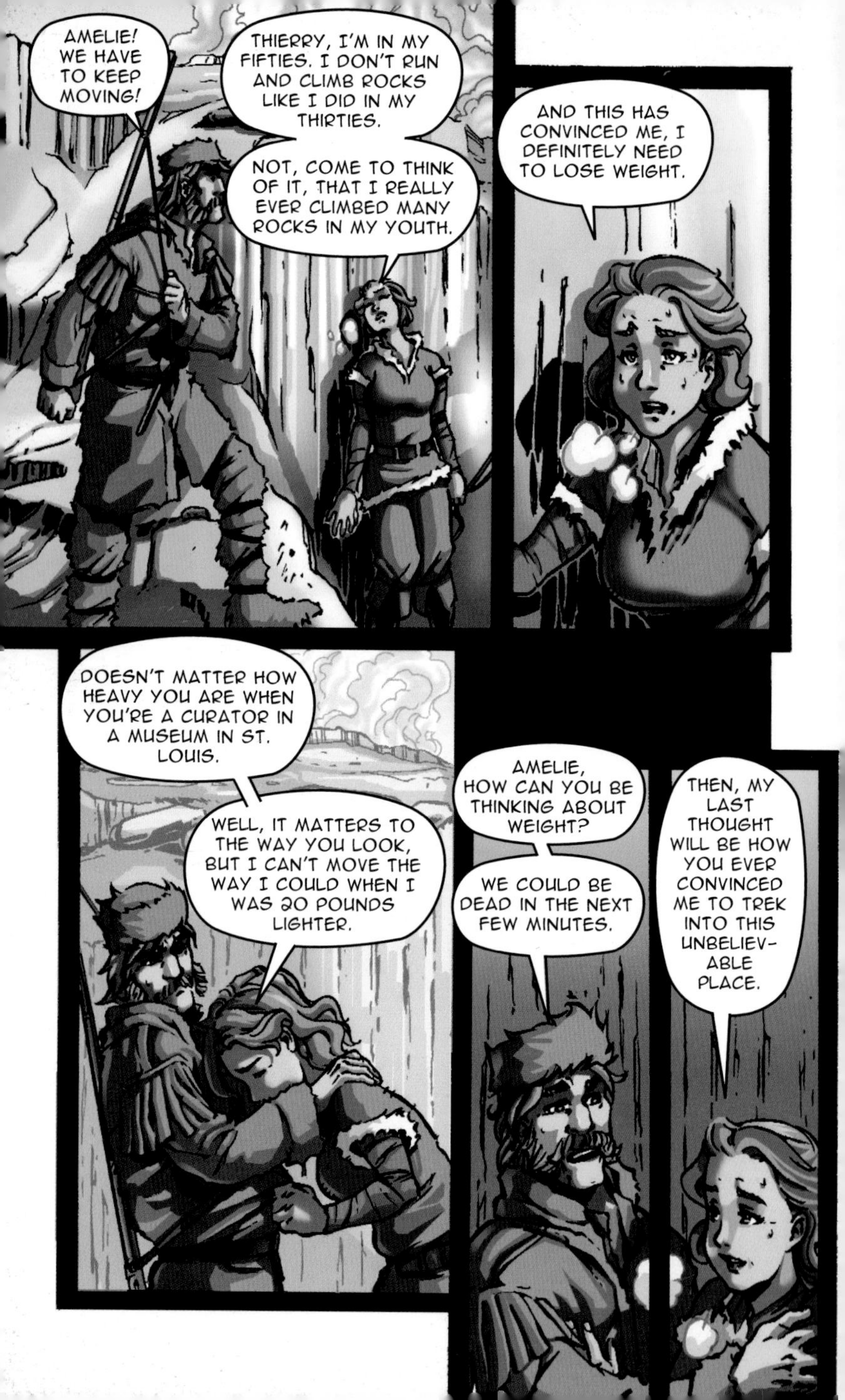
AMELIE! WE HAVE TO KEEP MOVING!
THIERRY, I'M IN MY FIFTIES. I DON'T RUN AND CLIMB ROCKS LIKE I DID IN MY THIRTIES.
NOT, COME TO THINK OF IT, THAT I REALLY EVER CLIMBED MANY ROCKS IN MY YOUTH.
AND THIS HAS CONVINCED ME, I DEFINITELY NEED TO LOSE WEIGHT.
DOESN'T MATTER HOW HEAVY YOU ARE WHEN YOU'RE A CURATOR IN A MUSEUM IN ST. LOUIS.
WELL, IT MATTERS TO THE WAY YOU LOOK, BUT I CAN'T MOVE THE WAY I COULD WHEN I WAS 20 POUNDS LIGHTER.
AMELIE, HOW CAN YOU BE THINKING ABOUT WEIGHT?
WE COULD BE DEAD IN THE NEXT FEW MINUTES.
THEN, MY LAST THOUGHT WILL BE HOW YOU EVER CONVINCED ME TO TREK INTO THIS UNBELIEV-ABLE PLACE.

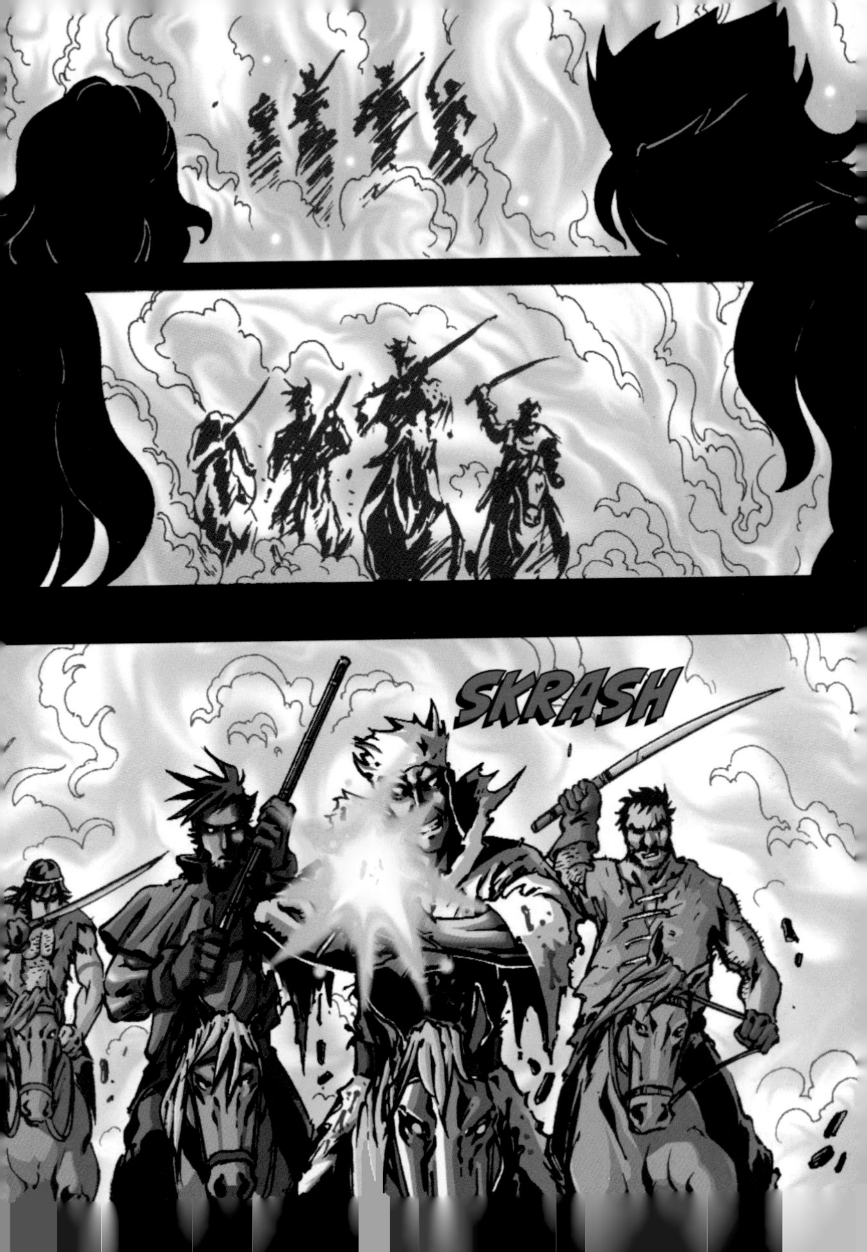
SKRASH

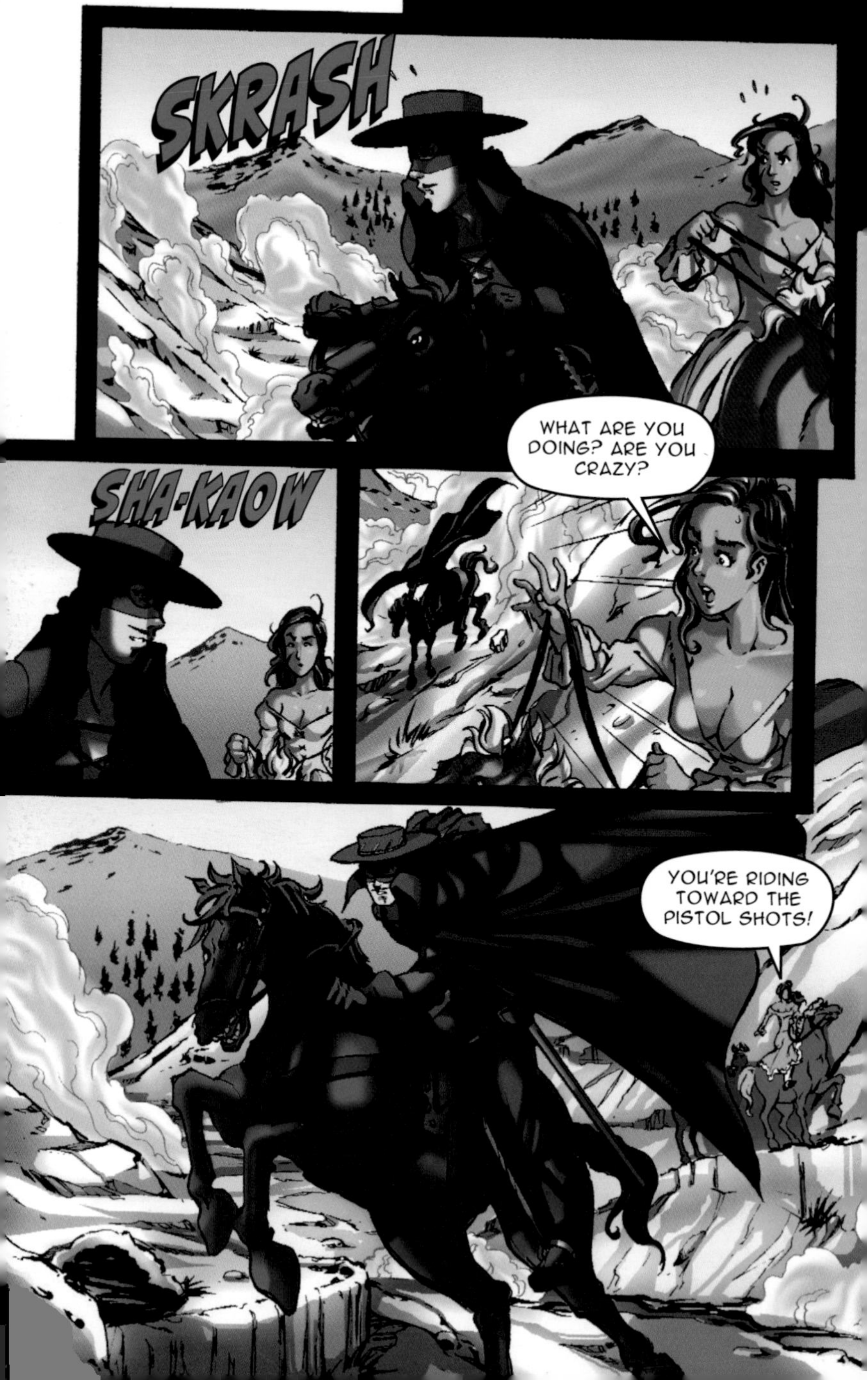
SKRASH
SHA-KAOW
WHAT ARE YOU DOING? ARE YOU CRAZY?
YOU'RE RIDING TOWARD THE PISTOL SHOTS!

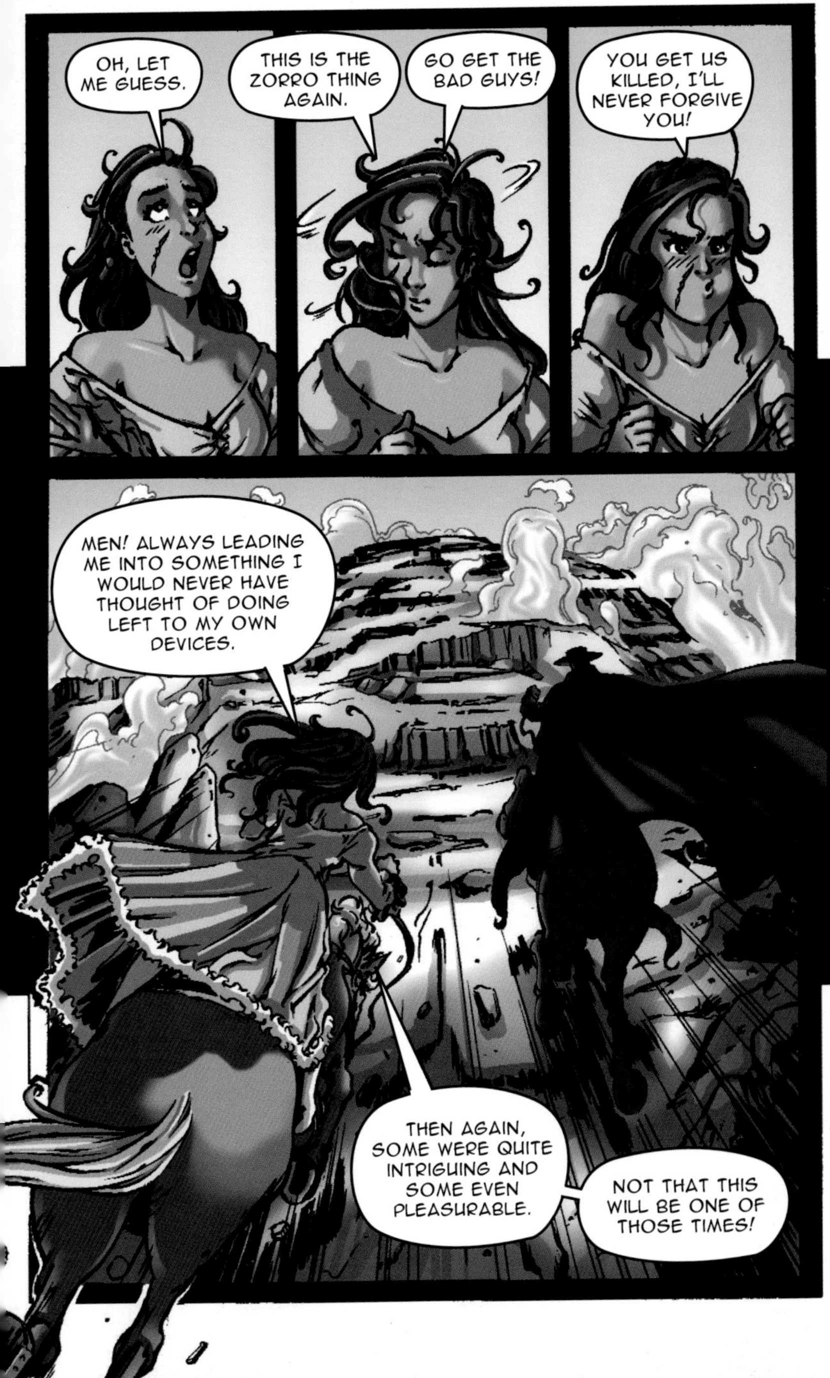

OH, LET ME GUESS.
THIS IS THE ZORRO THING AGAIN.
GO GET THE BAD GUYS!
YOU GET US KILLED, I'LL NEVER FORGIVE YOU!
MEN! ALWAYS LEADING ME INTO SOMETHING I WOULD NEVER HAVE THOUGHT OF DOING LEFT TO MY OWN DEVICES.
THEN AGAIN, SOME WERE QUITE INTRIGUING AND SOME EVEN PLEASURABLE.
NOT THAT THIS WILL BE ONE OF THOSE TIMES!

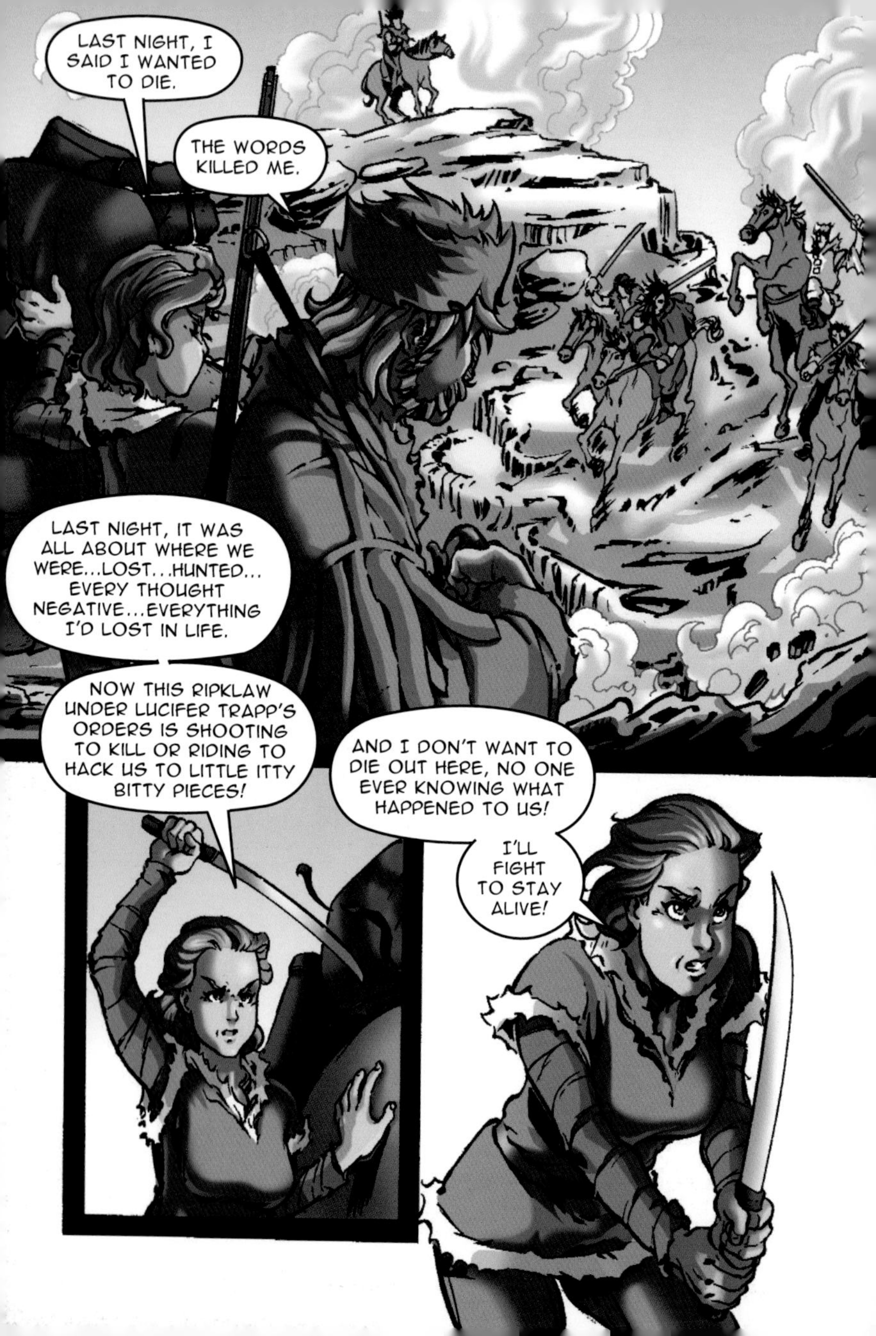
LAST NIGHT, I SAID I WANTED TO DIE.
THE WORDS KILLED ME.
LAST NIGHT, IT WAS ALL ABOUT WHERE WE WERE...LOST...HUNTED... EVERY THOUGHT NEGATIVE...EVERYTHING I'D LOST IN LIFE.
NOW THIS RIPKLAW UNDER LUCIFER TRAPP'S ORDERS IS SHOOTING TO KILL OR RIDING TO HACK US TO LITTLE ITTY BITTY PIECES!
AND I DON'T WANT TO DIE OUT HERE, NO ONE EVER KNOWING WHAT HAPPENED TO US!
I'LL FIGHT TO STAY ALIVE!

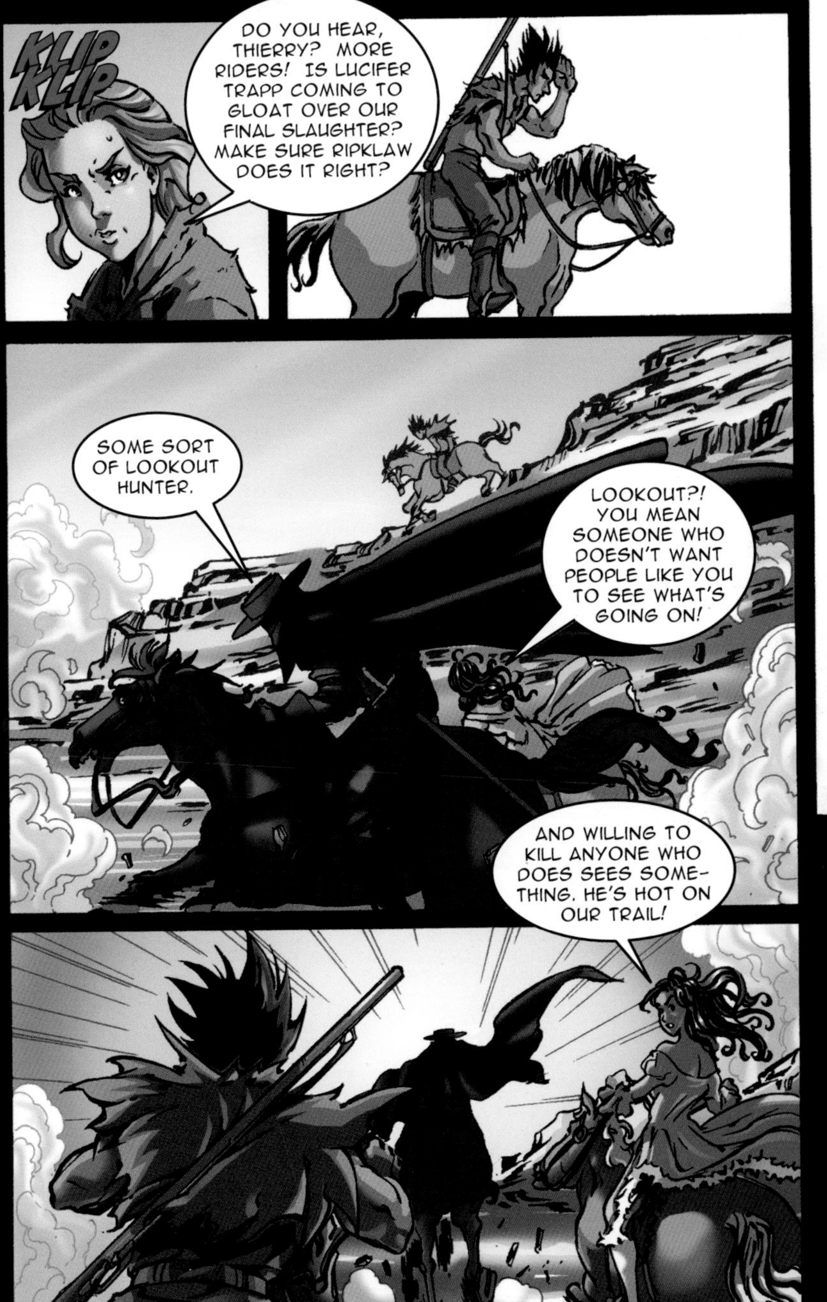
KLIP KLIP
DO YOU HEAR, THIERRY? MORE RIDERS! IS LUCIFER TRAPP COMING TO GLOAT OVER OUR FINAL SLAUGHTER? MAKE SURE RIPKLAW DOES IT RIGHT?
SOME SORT OF LOOKOUT HUNTER.
LOOKOUT?! YOU MEAN SOMEONE WHO DOESN'T WANT PEOPLE LIKE YOU TO SEE WHAT'S GOING ON!
AND WILLING TO KILL ANYONE WHO DOES SEES SOME-THING. HE'S HOT ON OUR TRAIL!

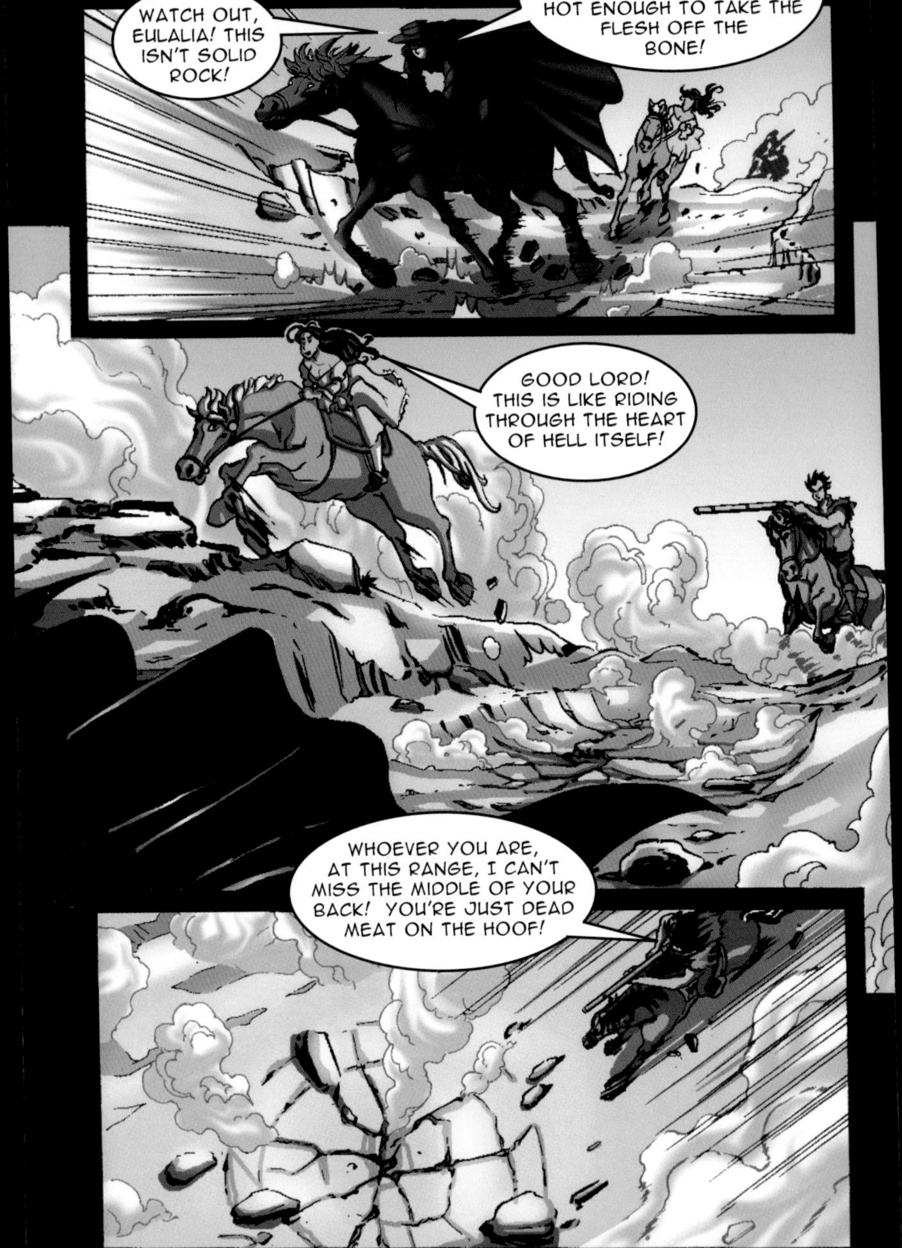
WATCH OUT, EULALIA! THIS ISN'T SOLID ROCK!
IT'S LITTLE MORE THAN A THIN ROCKY CRUST OVER A BOILING CAULDRON HOT ENOUGH TO TAKE THE FLESH OFF THE BONE!
GOOD LORD! THIS IS LIKE RIDING THROUGH THE HEART OF HELL ITSELF!
WHOEVER YOU ARE, AT THIS RANGE, I CAN'T MISS THE MIDDLE OF YOUR BACK! YOU'RE JUST DEAD MEAT ON THE HOOF!

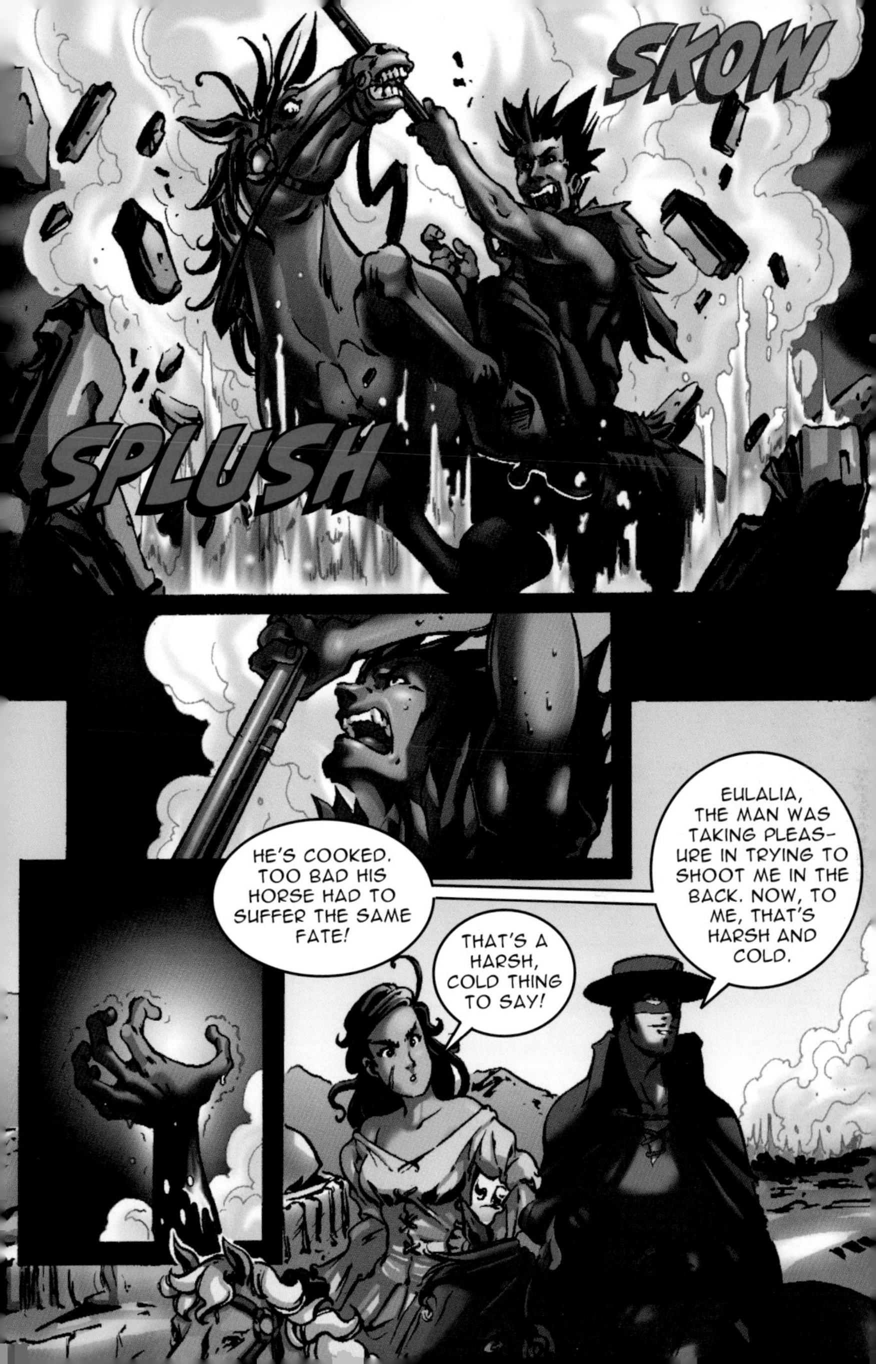
SKOW
SPLUSH
HE'S COOKED. TOO BAD HIS HORSE HAD TO SUFFER THE SAME FATE!
THAT'S A HARSH, COLD THING TO SAY!
EULALIA, THE MAN WAS TAKING PLEAS-URE IN TRYING TO SHOOT ME IN THE BACK. NOW, TO ME, THAT'S HARSH AND COLD.

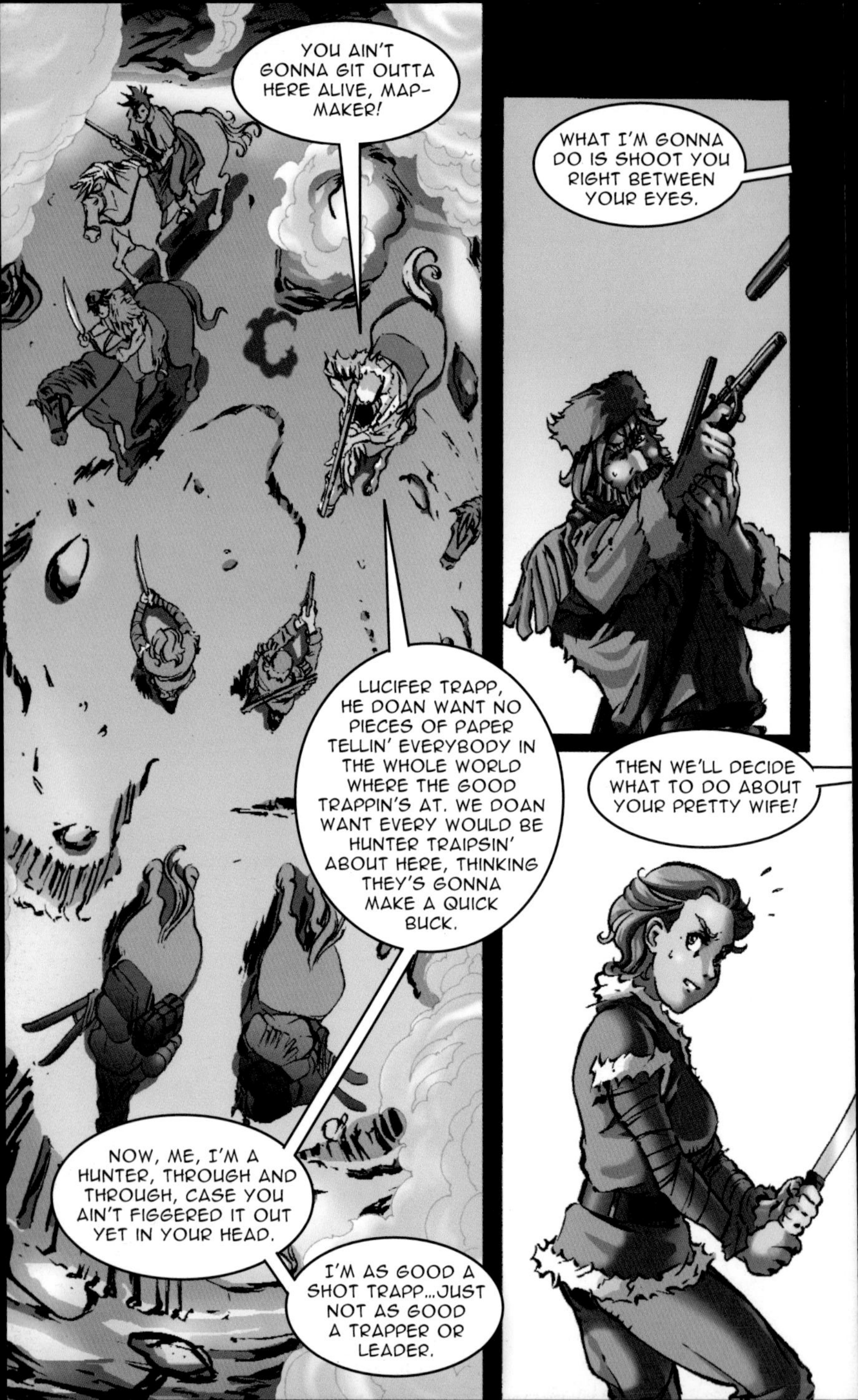
YOU AIN'T GONNA GIT OUTTA HERE ALIVE, MAP-MAKER!
LUCIFER TRAPP, HE DOAN WANT NO PIECES OF PAPER TELLIN' EVERYBODY IN THE WHOLE WORLD WHERE THE GOOD TRAPPIN'S AT. WE DOAN WANT EVERY WOULD BE HUNTER TRAIPSIN' ABOUT HERE, THINKING THEY'S GONNA MAKE A QUICK BUCK.
NOW, ME, I'M A HUNTER, THROUGH AND THROUGH, CASE YOU AIN'T FIGGERED IT OUT YET IN YOUR HEAD.
I'M AS GOOD A SHOT TRAPP...JUST NOT AS GOOD A TRAPPER OR LEADER.
WHAT I'M GONNA DO IS SHOOT YOU RIGHT BETWEEN YOUR EYES.
THEN WE'LL DECIDE WHAT TO DO ABOUT YOUR PRETTY WIFE!

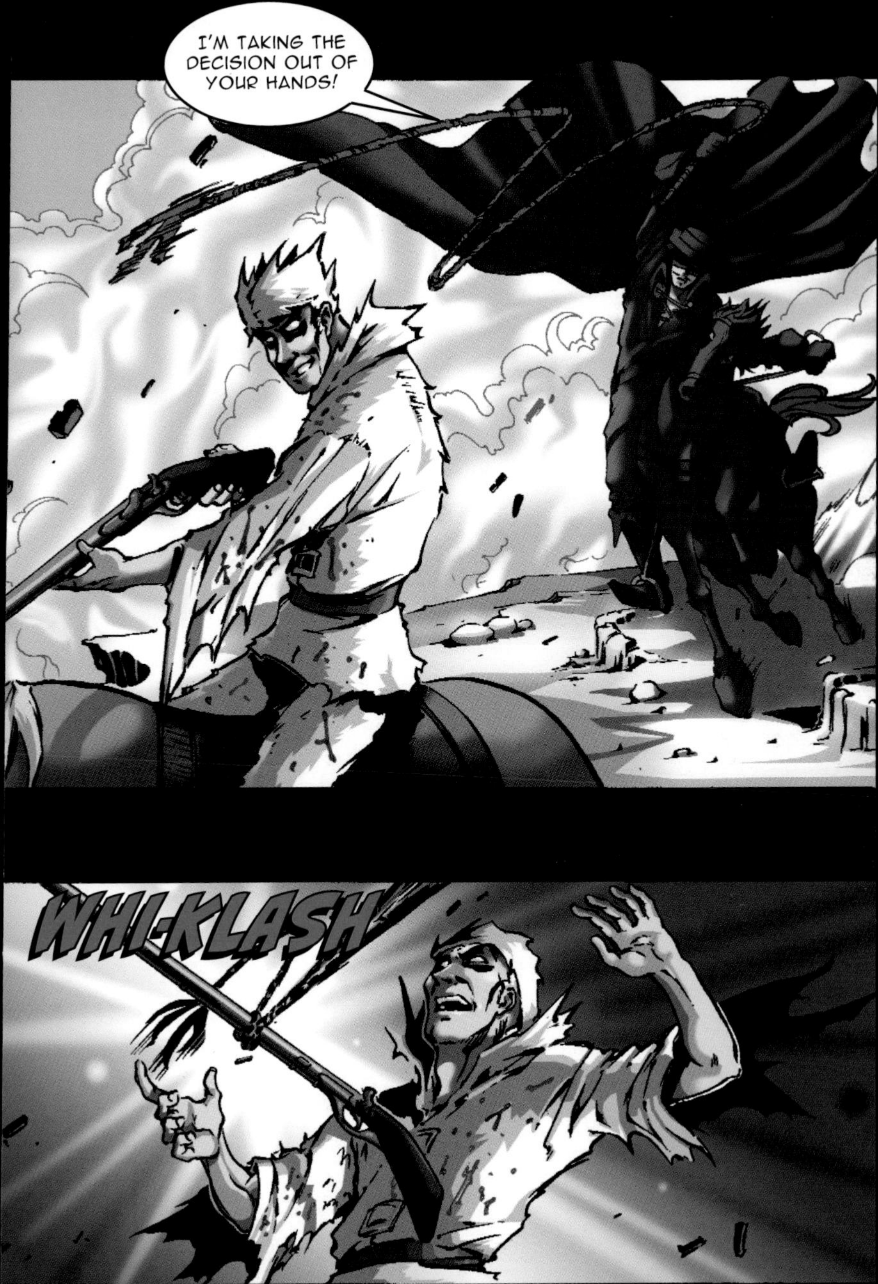
I'M TAKING THE DECISION OUT OF YOUR HANDS!
WHI-KLASH

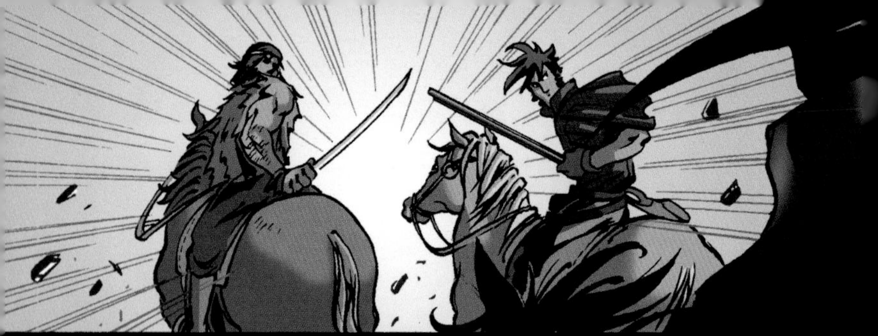
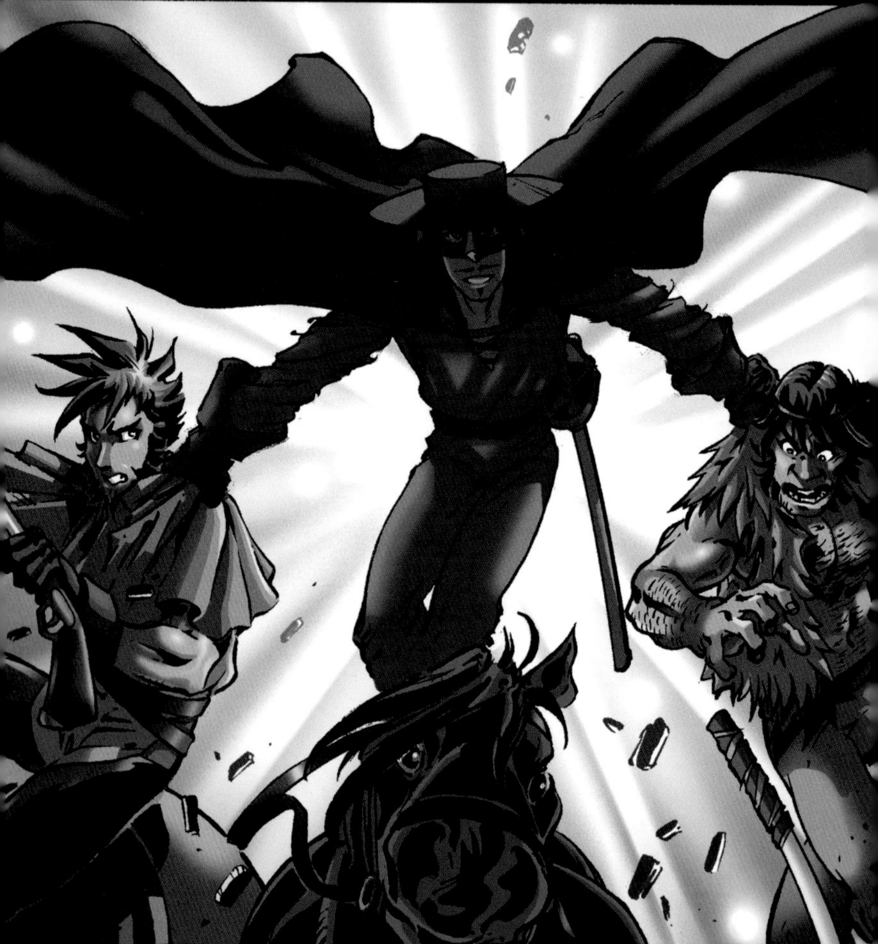

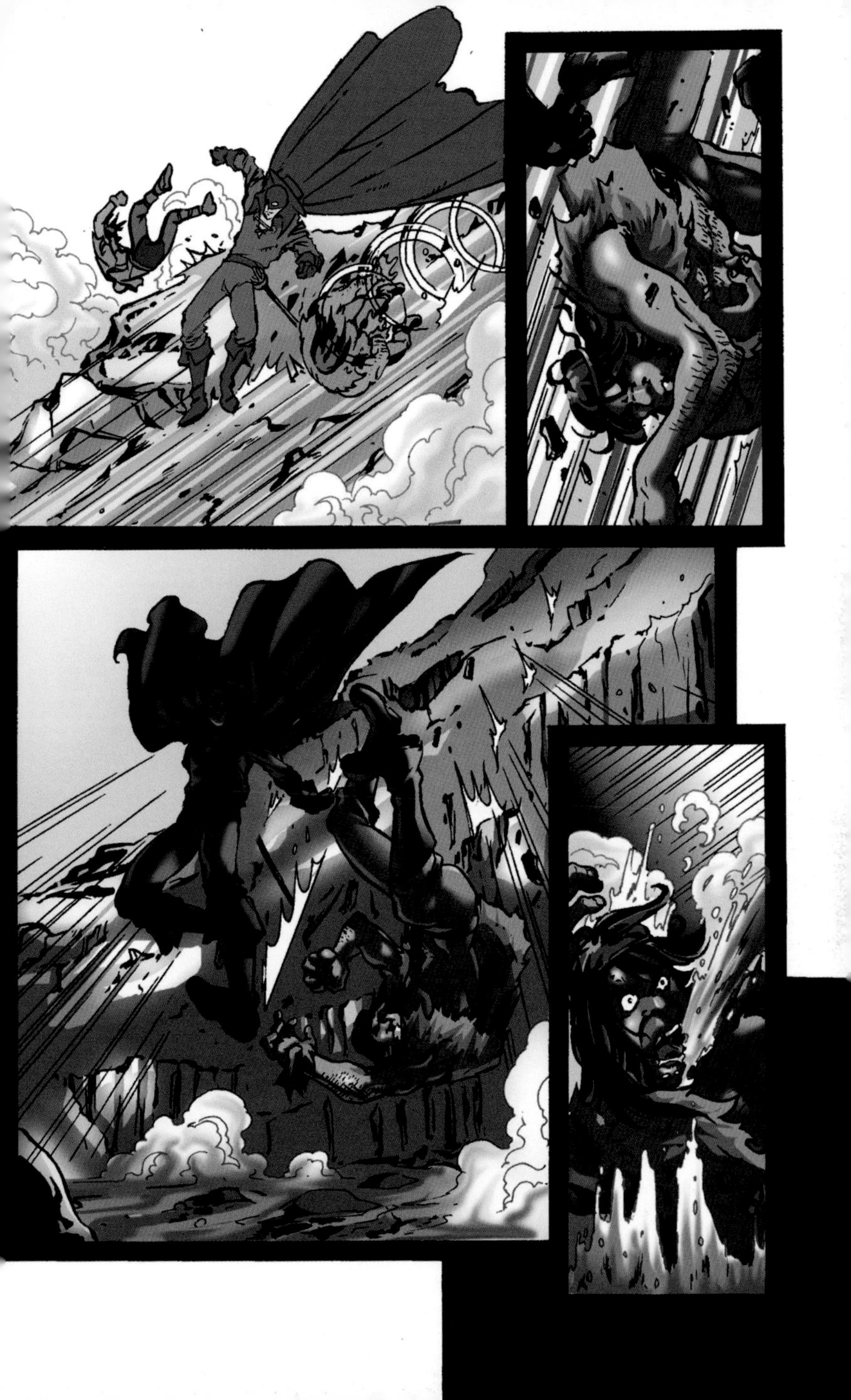

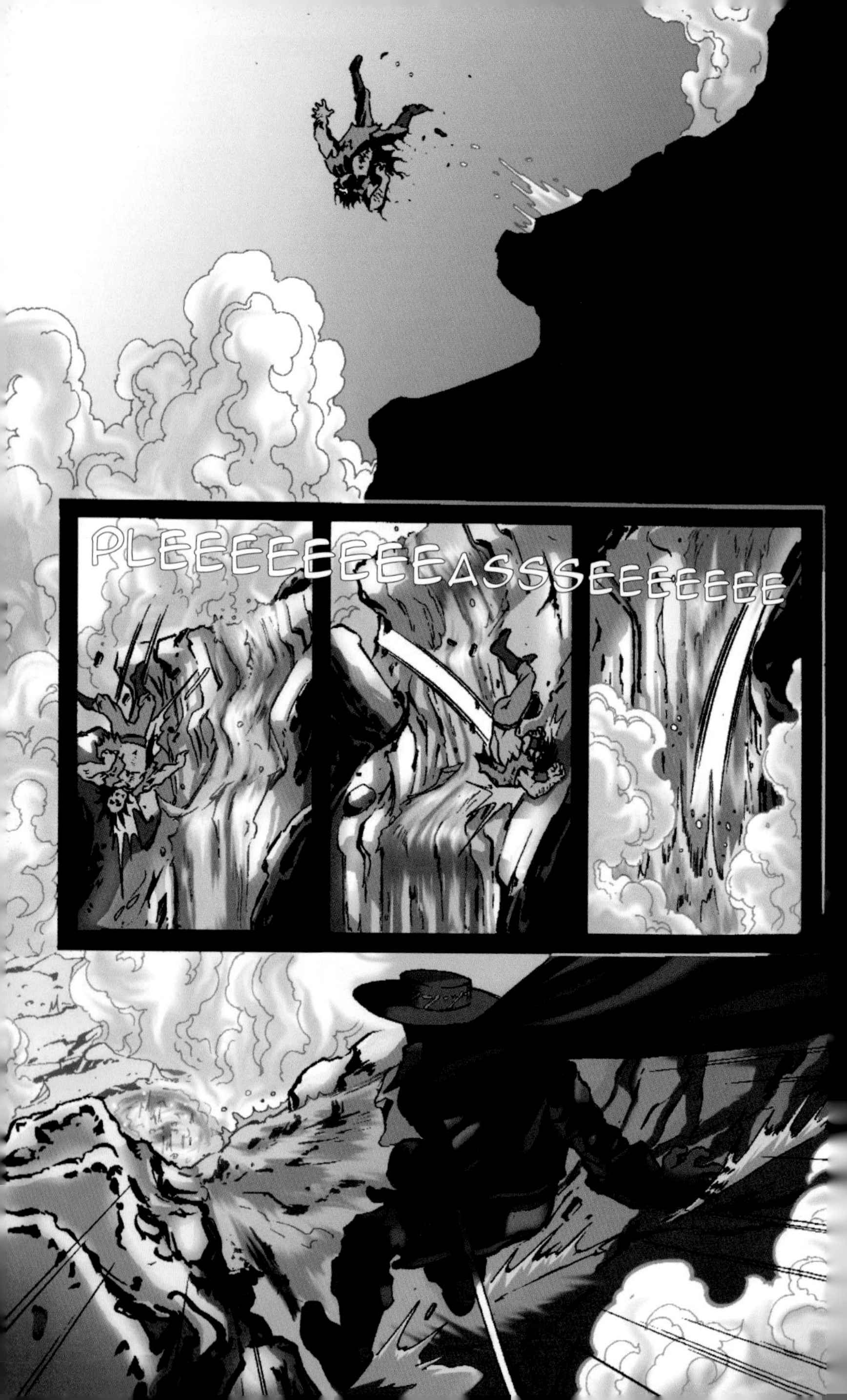
PLEEEEEEEEEASSSEEEEEEEE

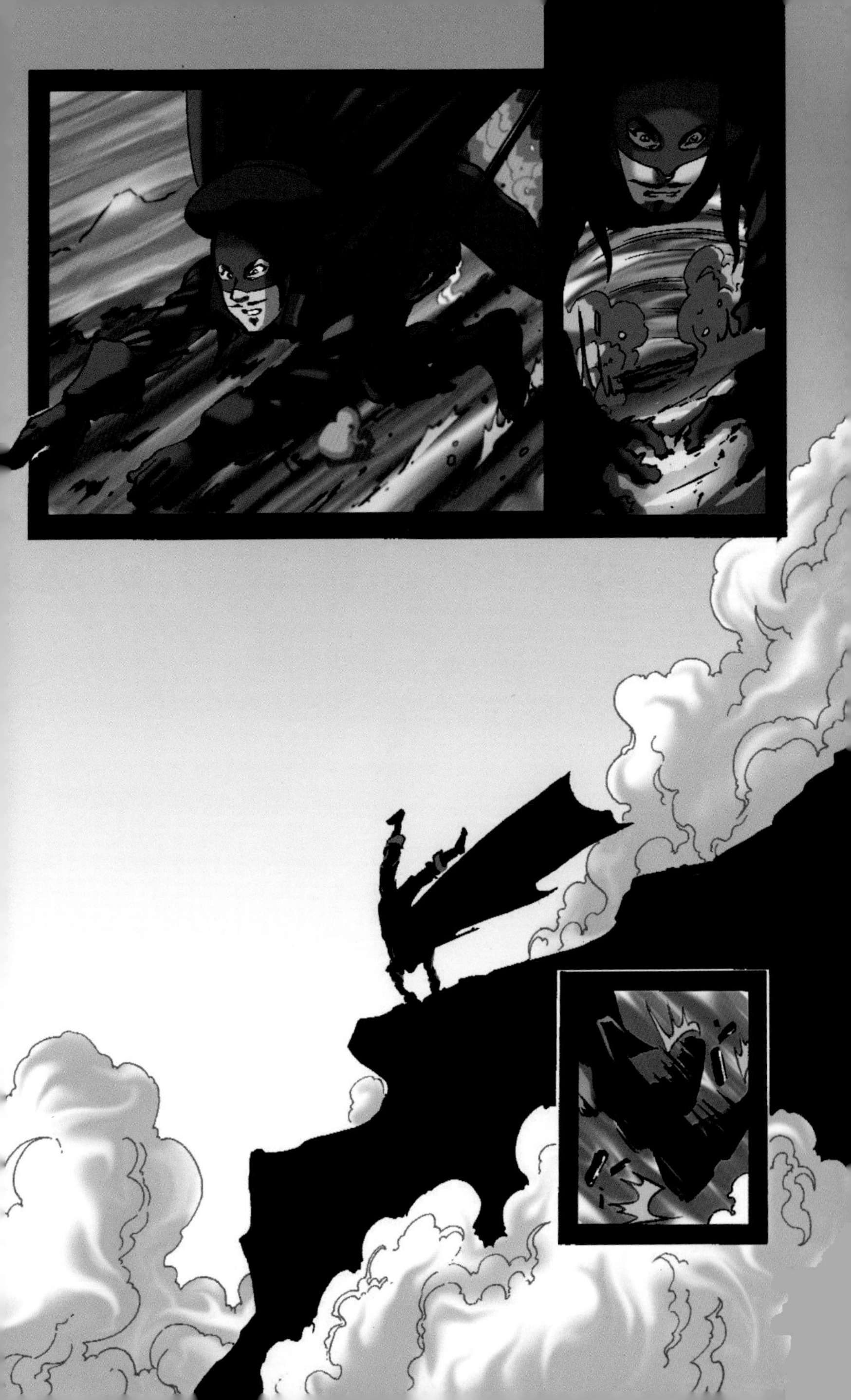

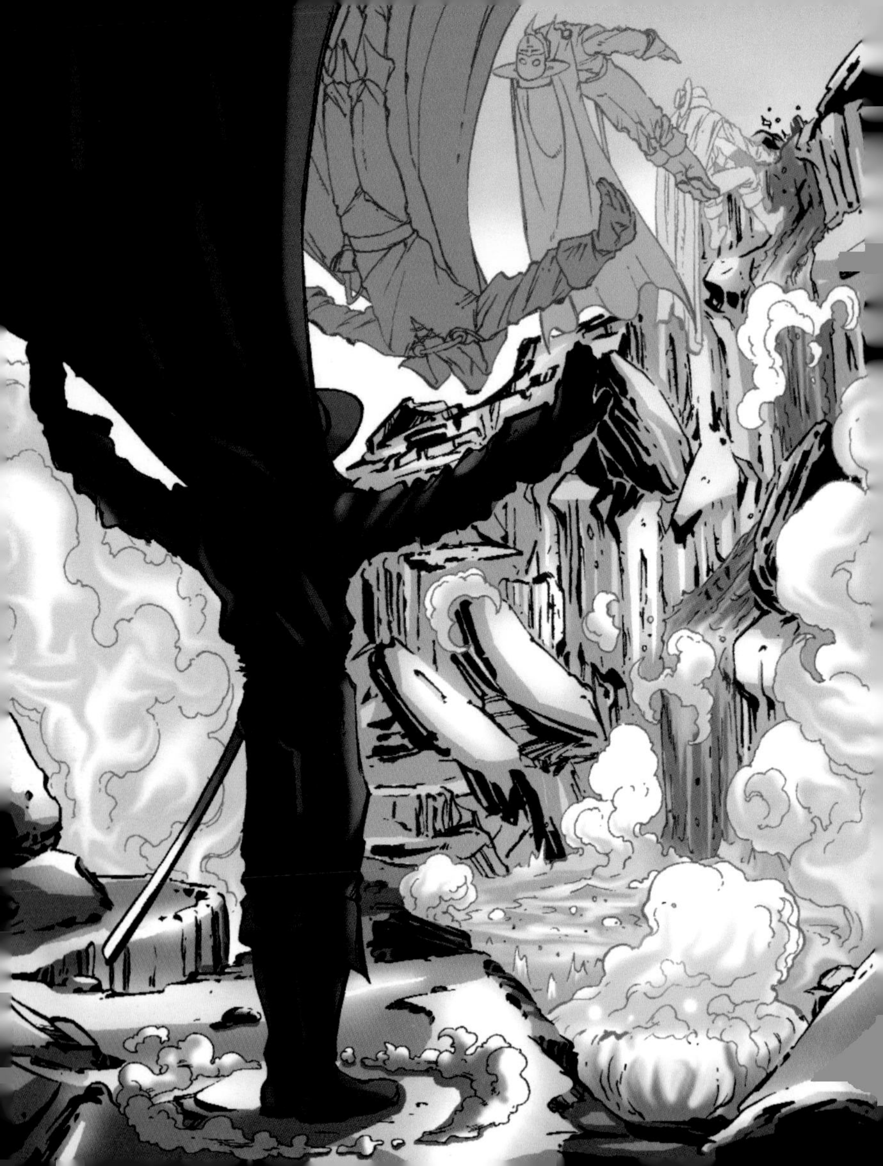

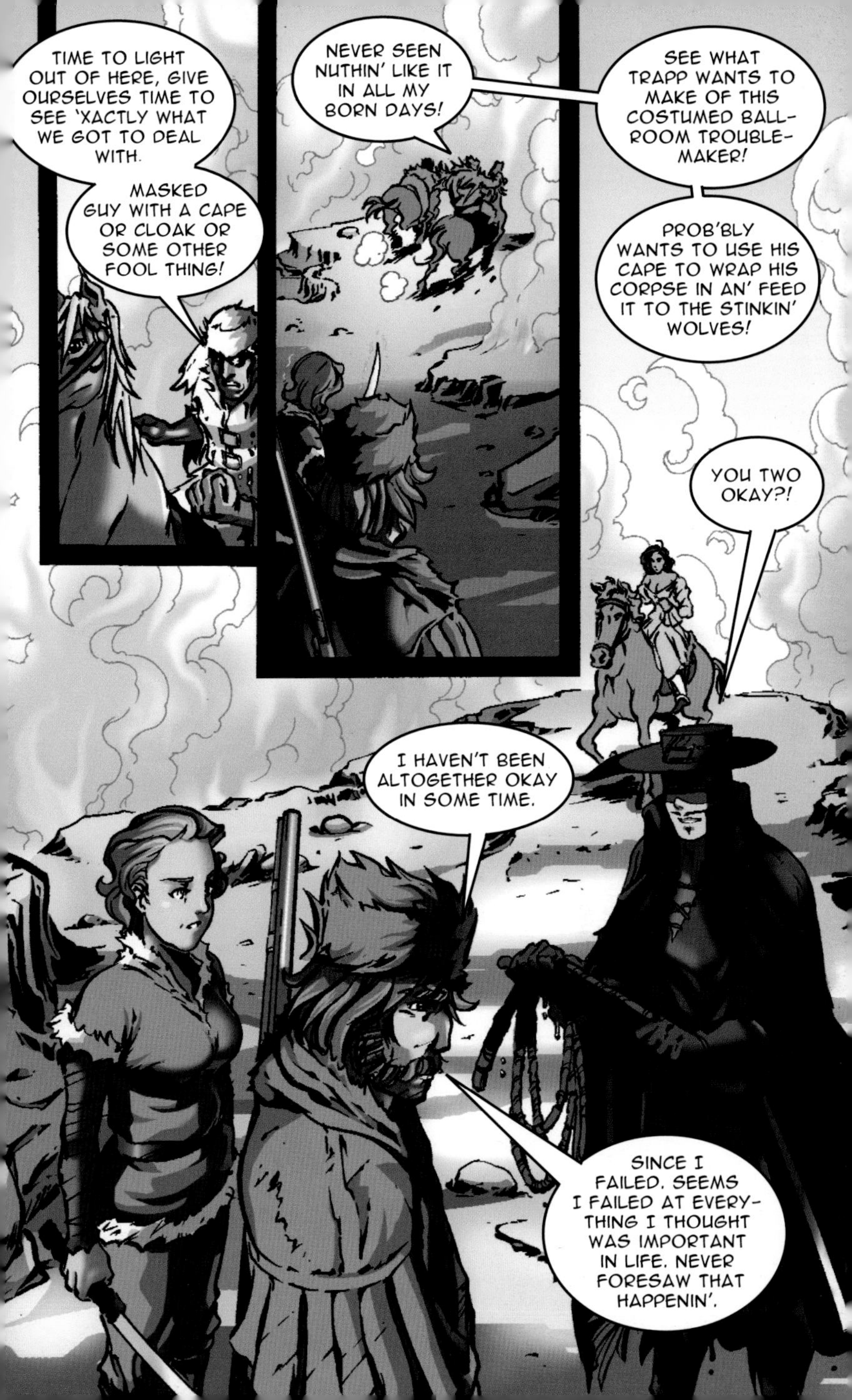
TIME TO LIGHT OUT OF HERE, GIVE OURSELVES TIME TO SEE 'XACTLY WHAT WE GOT TO DEAL WITH.
MASKED GUY WITH A CAPE OR CLOAK OR SOME OTHER FOOL THING!
NEVER SEEN NUTHIN' LIKE IT IN ALL MY BORN DAYS!
SEE WHAT TRAPP WANTS TO MAKE OF THIS COSTUMED BALL-ROOM TROUBLE-MAKER!
PROB'BLY WANTS TO USE HIS CAPE TO WRAP HIS CORPSE IN AN' FEED IT TO THE STINKIN' WOLVES!
YOU TWO OKAY?!
I HAVEN'T BEEN ALTOGETHER OKAY IN SOME TIME.
SINCE I FAILED. SEEMS I FAILED AT EVERY-THING I THOUGHT WAS IMPORTANT IN LIFE. NEVER FORESAW THAT HAPPENIN'.

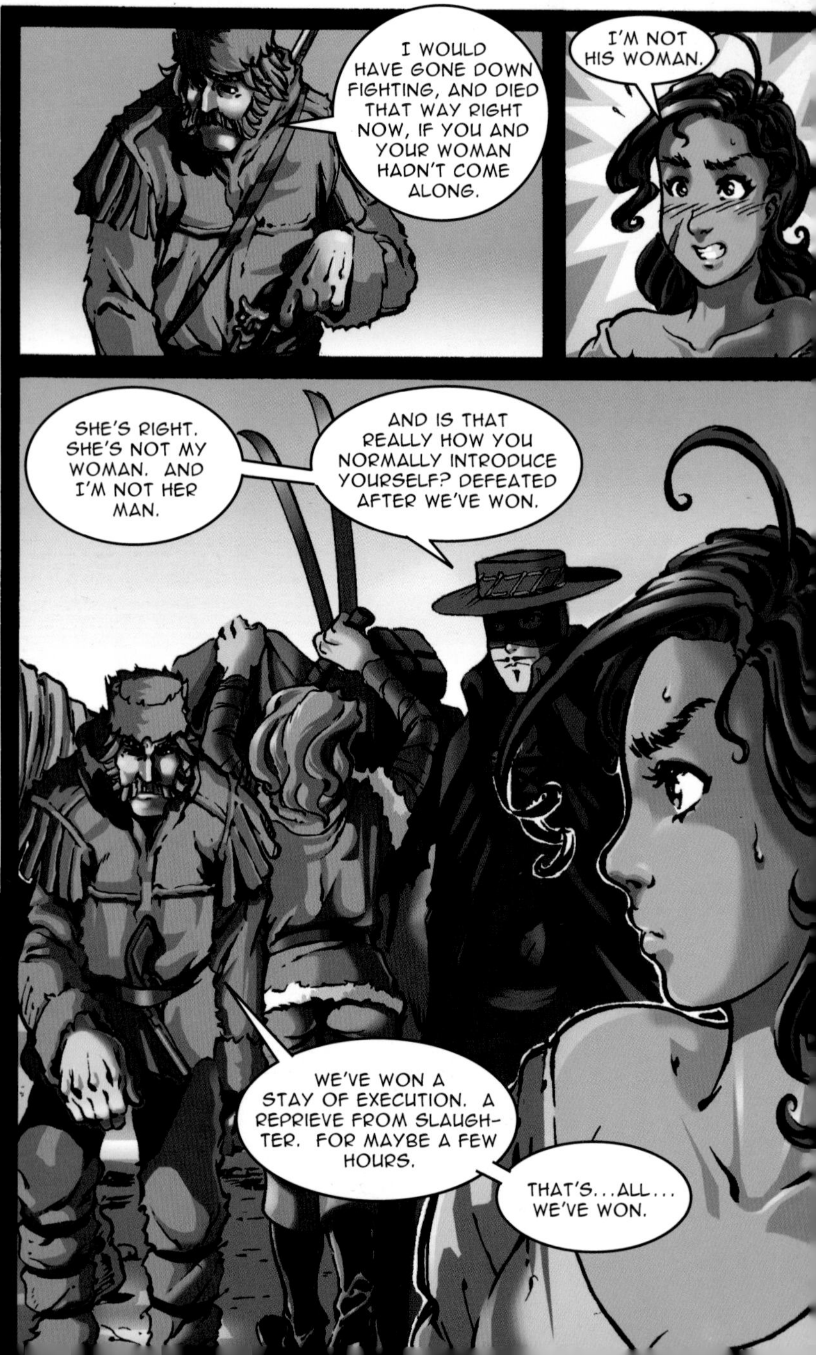
I WOULD HAVE GONE DOWN FIGHTING, AND DIED THAT WAY RIGHT NOW, IF YOU AND YOUR WOMAN HADN'T COME ALONG.
I'M NOT HIS WOMAN.
SHE'S RIGHT. SHE'S NOT MY WOMAN. AND I'M NOT HER MAN.
AND IS THAT REALLY HOW YOU NORMALLY INTRODUCE YOURSELF? DEFEATED AFTER WE'VE WON.
WE'VE WON A STAY OF EXECUTION. A REPRIEVE FROM SLAUGH-TER. FOR MAYBE A FEW HOURS.
THAT'S...ALL... WE'VE WON.

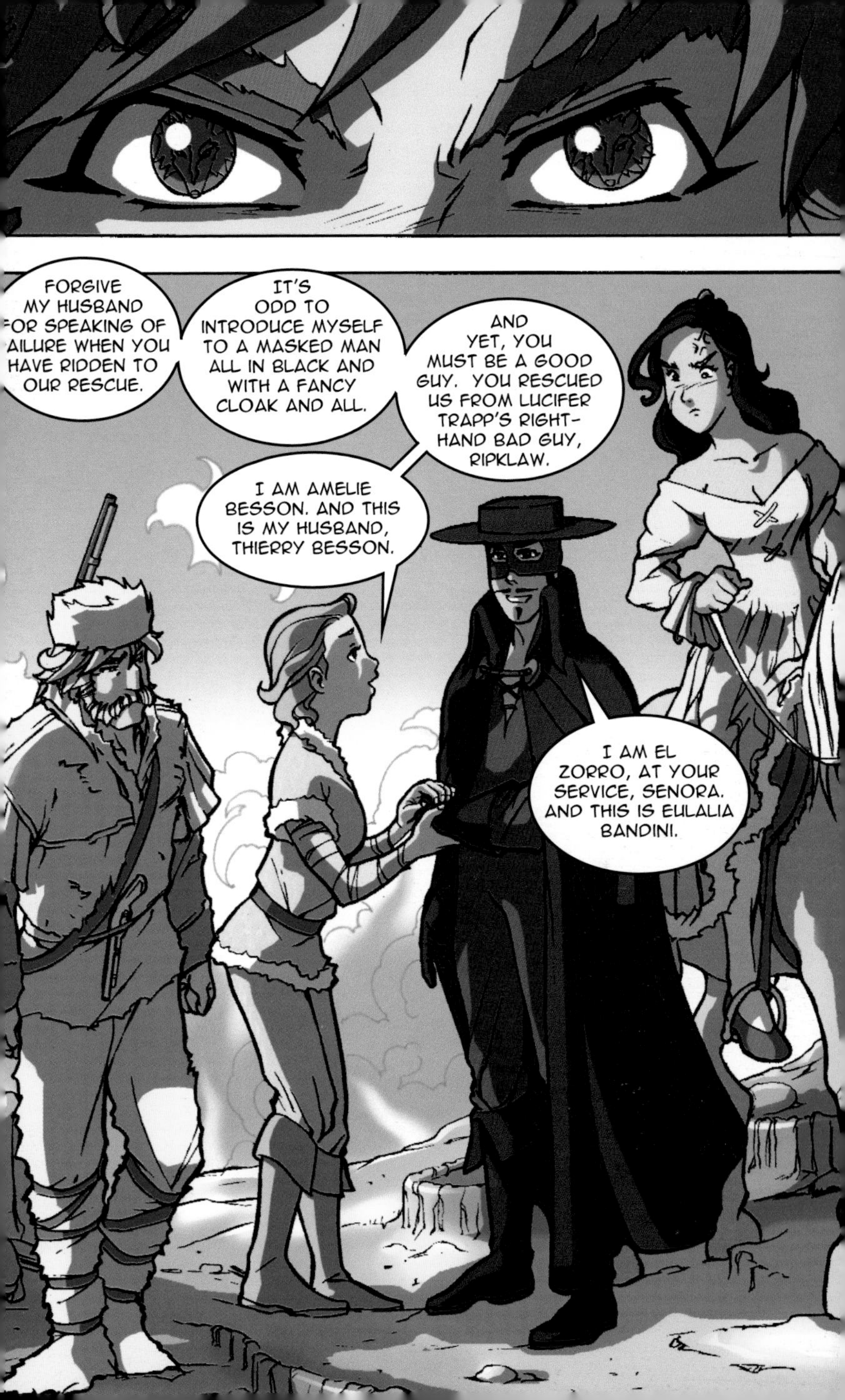
FORGIVE MY HUSBAND FOR SPEAKING OF AILURE WHEN YOU HAVE RIDDEN TO OUR RESCUE.
IT'S ODD TO INTRODUCE MYSELF TO A MASKED MAN ALL IN BLACK AND WITH A FANCY CLOAK AND ALL.
AND YET, YOU MUST BE A GOOD GUY. YOU RESCUED US FROM LUCIFER TRAPP'S RIGHT-HAND BAD GUY, RIPKLAW.
I AM AMELIE BESSON. AND THIS IS MY HUSBAND, THIERRY BESSON.
I AM EL ZORRO, AT YOUR SERVICE, SENORA. AND THIS IS EULALIA BANDINI.

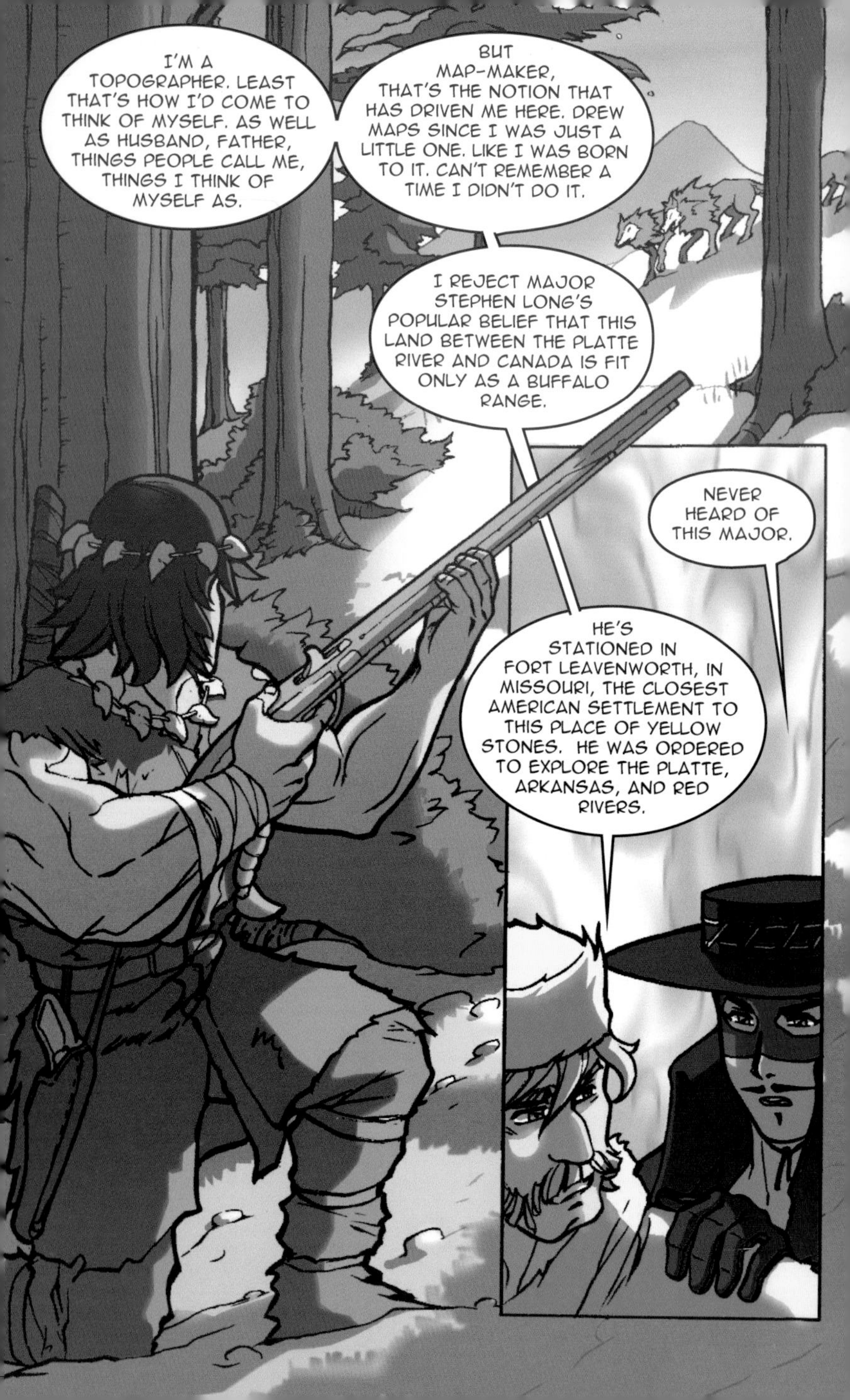
I'M A TOPOGRAPHER. LEAST THAT'S HOW I'D COME TO THINK OF MYSELF. AS WELL AS HUSBAND, FATHER, THINGS PEOPLE CALL ME, THINGS I THINK OF MYSELF AS.
BUT MAP-MAKER, THAT'S THE NOTION THAT HAS DRIVEN ME HERE. DREW MAPS SINCE I WAS JUST A LITTLE ONE. LIKE I WAS BORN TO IT. CAN'T REMEMBER A TIME I DIDN'T DO IT.
I REJECT MAJOR STEPHEN LONG'S POPULAR BELIEF THAT THIS LAND BETWEEN THE PLATTE RIVER AND CANADA IS FIT ONLY AS A BUFFALO RANGE.
NEVER HEARD OF THIS MAJOR.
HE'S STATIONED IN FORT LEAVENWORTH, IN MISSOURI, THE CLOSEST AMERICAN SETTLEMENT TO THIS PLACE OF YELLOW STONES. HE WAS ORDERED TO EXPLORE THE PLATTE, ARKANSAS, AND RED RIVERS.

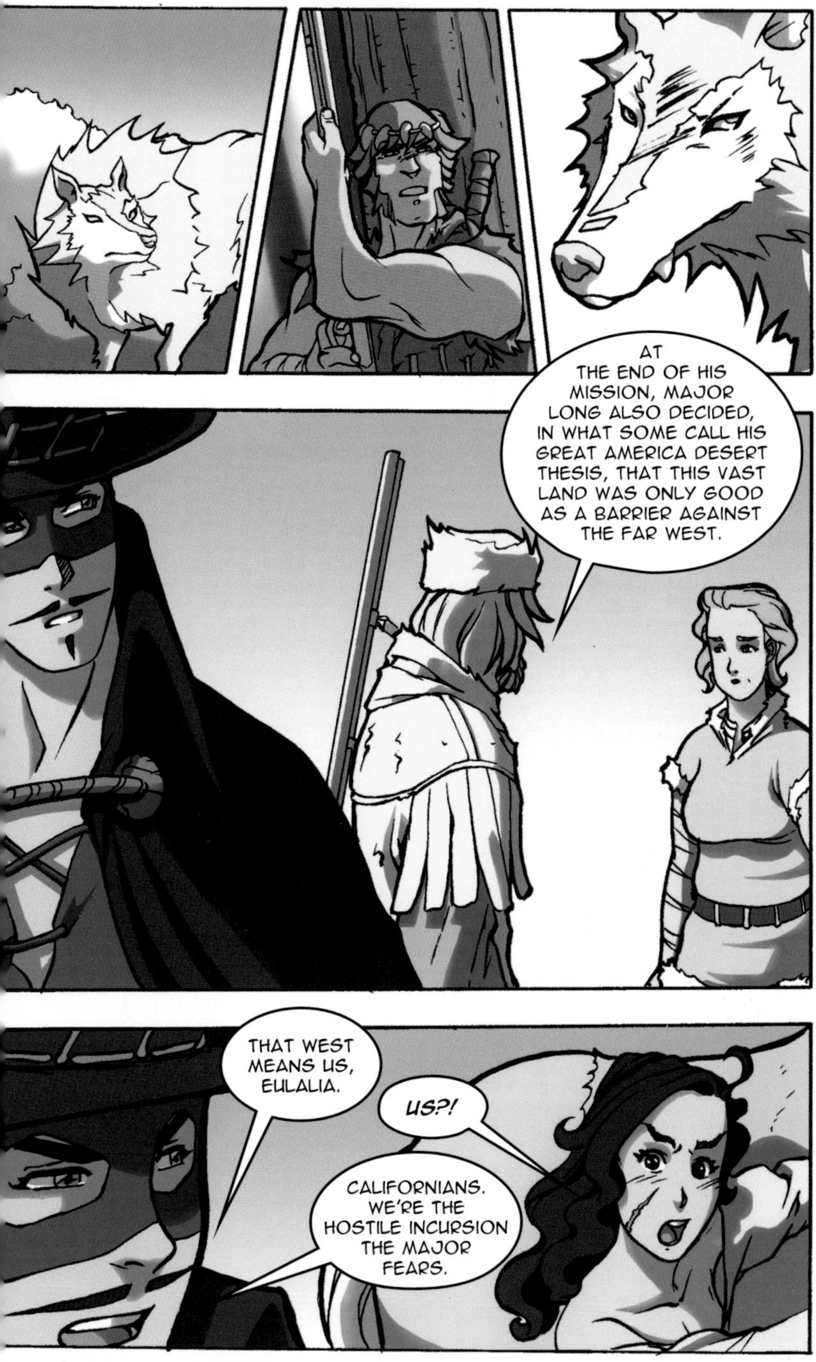
AT THE END OF HIS MISSION, MAJOR LONG ALSO DECIDED, IN WHAT SOME CALL HIS GREAT AMERICA DESERT THESIS, THAT THIS VAST LAND WAS ONLY GOOD AS A BARRIER AGAINST THE FAR WEST.
THAT WEST MEANS US, EULALIA.
US?!
CALIFORNIANS. WE'RE THE HOSTILE INCURSION THE MAJOR FEARS.

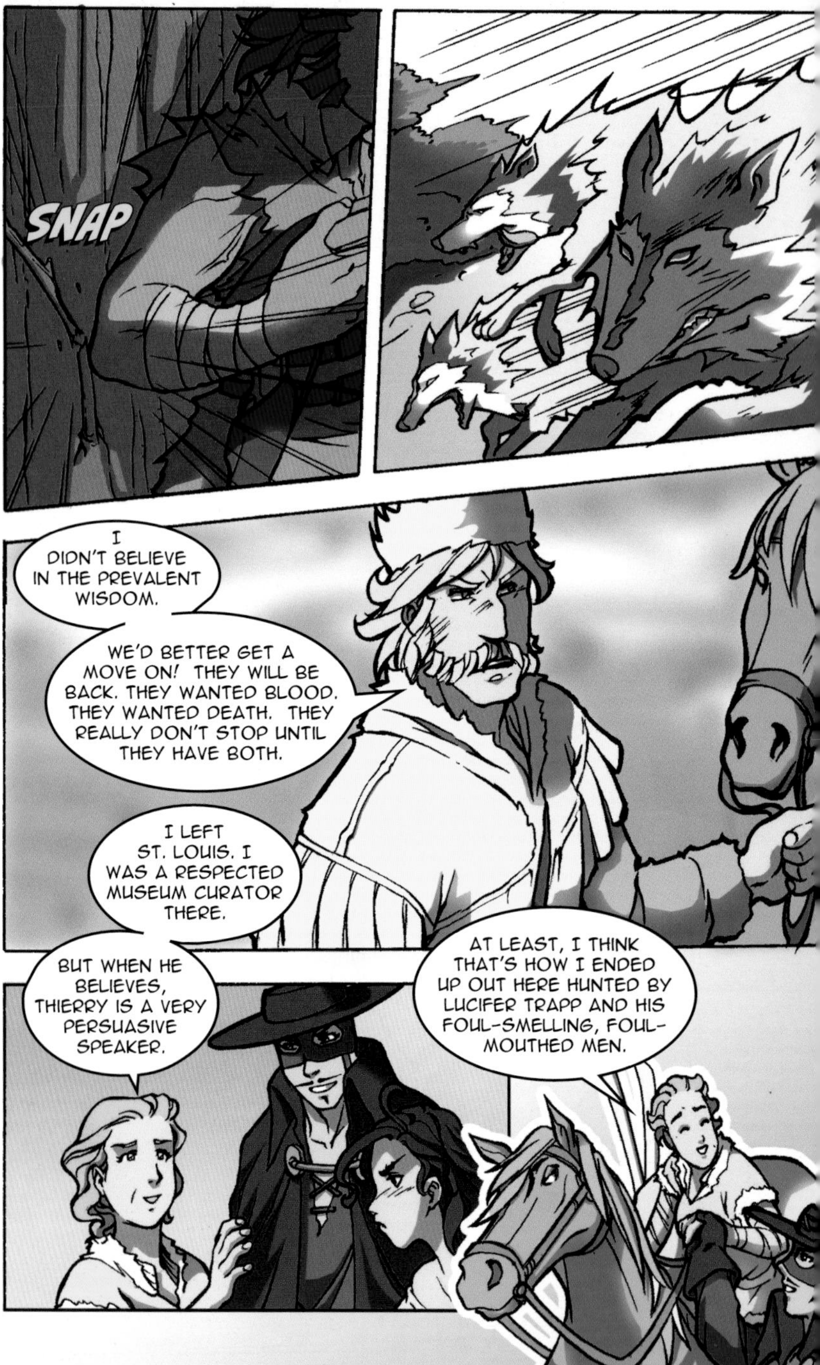
SNAP
I DIDN'T BELIEVE IN THE PREVALENT WISDOM.
WE'D BETTER GET A MOVE ON! THEY WILL BE BACK. THEY WANTED BLOOD. THEY WANTED DEATH. THEY REALLY DON'T STOP UNTIL THEY HAVE BOTH.
I LEFT ST. LOUIS. I WAS A RESPECTED MUSEUM CURATOR THERE.
BUT WHEN HE BELIEVES, THIERRY IS A VERY PERSUASIVE SPEAKER.
AT LEAST, I THINK THAT'S HOW I ENDED UP OUT HERE HUNTED BY LUCIFER TRAPP AND HIS FOUL-SMELLING, FOUL-MOUTHED MEN.

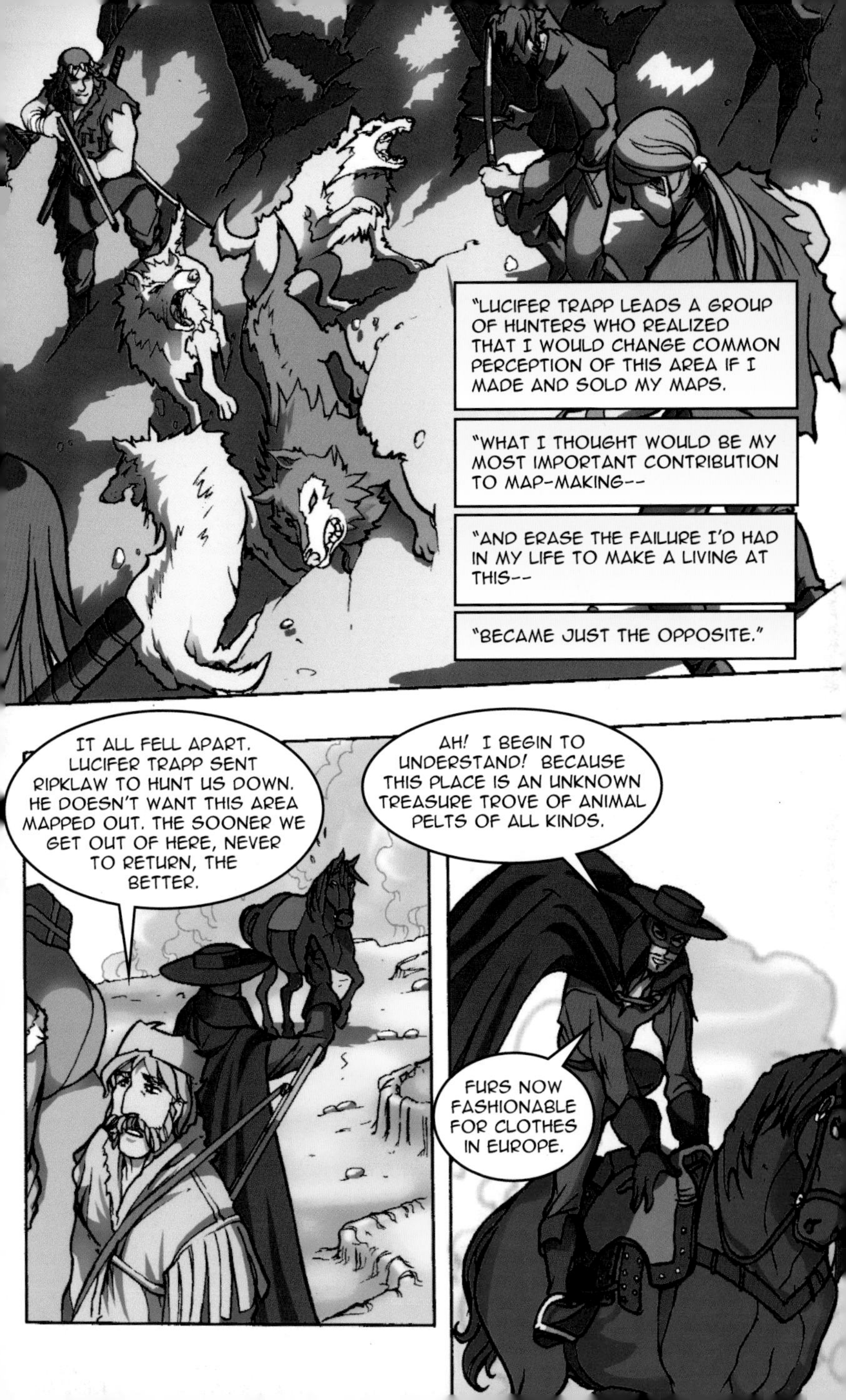
"LUCIFER TRAPP LEADS A GROUP OF HUNTERS WHO REALIZED THAT I WOULD CHANGE COMMON PERCEPTION OF THIS AREA IF I MADE AND SOLD MY MAPS.
"WHAT I THOUGHT WOULD BE MY MOST IMPORTANT CONTRIBUTION TO MAP-MAKING--
"AND ERASE THE FAILURE I'D HAD IN MY LIFE TO MAKE A LIVING AT THIS--
"BECAME JUST THE OPPOSITE."
IT ALL FELL APART. LUCIFER TRAPP SENT RIPKLAW TO HUNT US DOWN. HE DOESN'T WANT THIS AREA MAPPED OUT. THE SOONER WE GET OUT OF HERE, NEVER TO RETURN, THE BETTER.
AH! I BEGIN TO UNDERSTAND! BECAUSE THIS PLACE IS AN UNKNOWN TREASURE TROVE OF ANIMAL PELTS OF ALL KINDS.
FURS NOW FASHIONABLE FOR CLOTHES IN EUROPE.

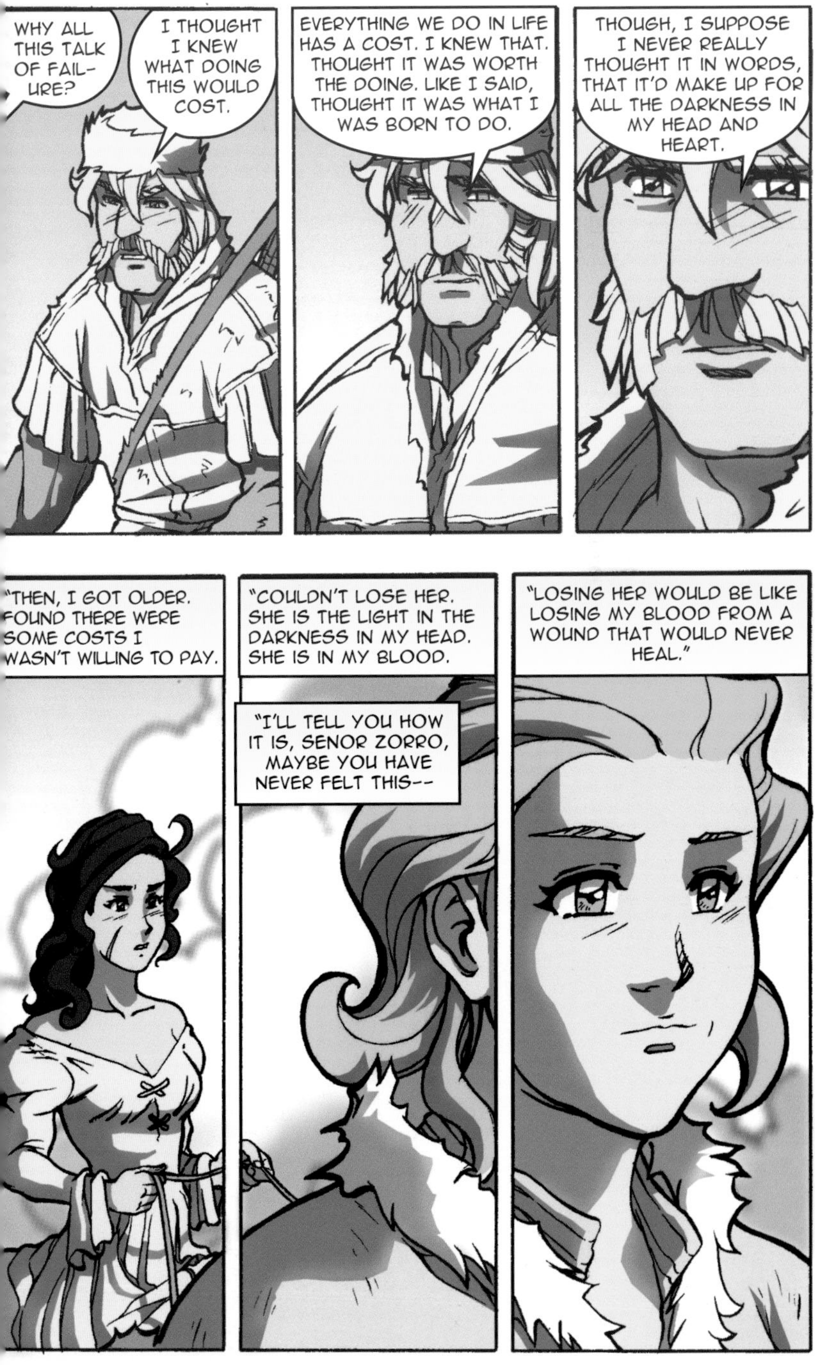
WHY ALL THIS TALK OF FAIL-URE?
I THOUGHT I KNEW WHAT DOING THIS WOULD COST.
EVERYTHING WE DO IN LIFE HAS A COST. I KNEW THAT. THOUGHT IT WAS WORTH THE DOING. LIKE I SAID, THOUGHT IT WAS WHAT I WAS BORN TO DO.
THOUGH, I SUPPOSE I NEVER REALLY THOUGHT IT IN WORDS, THAT IT'D MAKE UP FOR ALL THE DARKNESS IN MY HEAD AND HEART.
"THEN, I GOT OLDER. FOUND THERE WERE SOME COSTS I WASN'T WILLING TO PAY.
"COULDN'T LOSE HER. SHE IS THE LIGHT IN THE DARKNESS IN MY HEAD. SHE IS IN MY BLOOD.
"I'LL TELL YOU HOW IT IS, SENOR ZORRO, MAYBE YOU HAVE NEVER FELT THIS--
"LOSING HER WOULD BE LIKE LOSING MY BLOOD FROM A WOUND THAT WOULD NEVER HEAL."

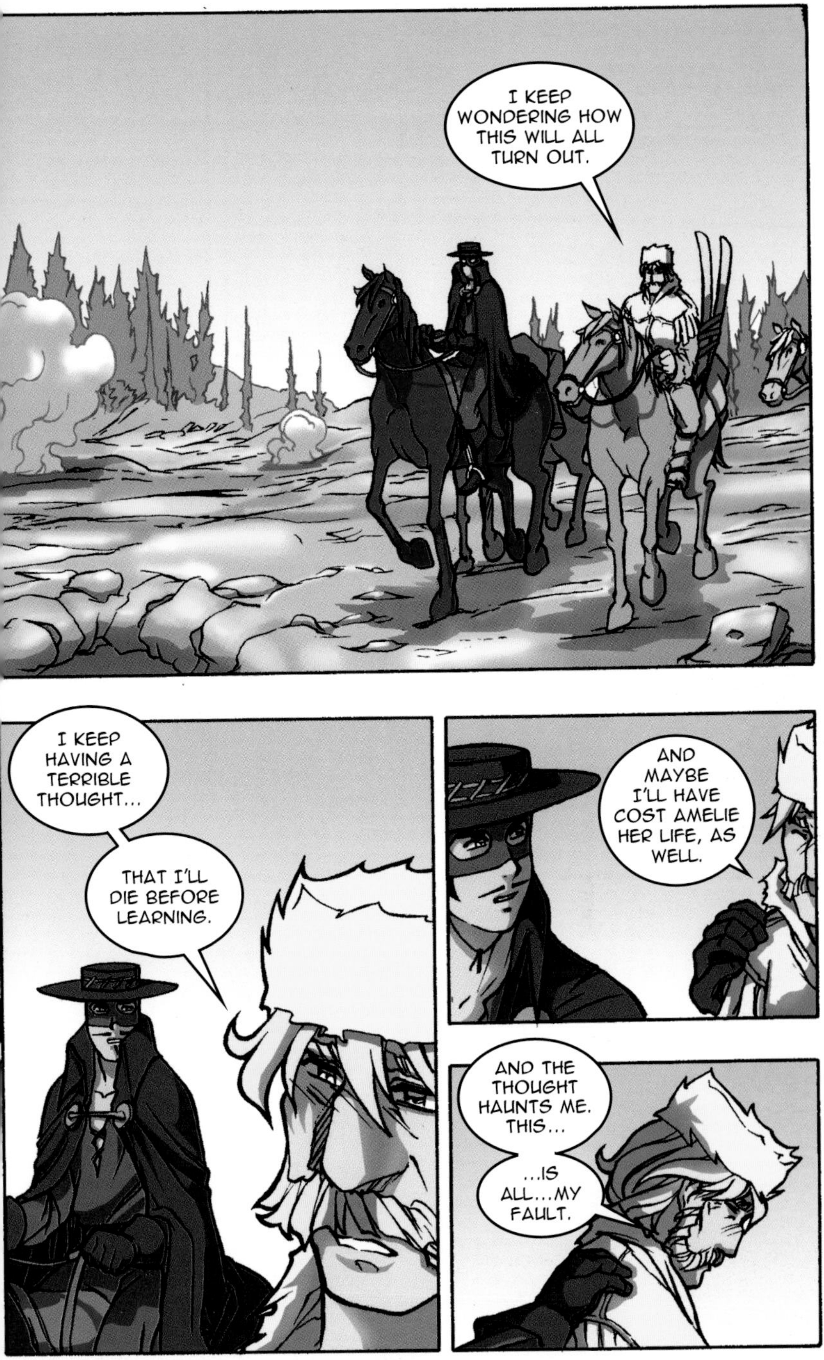
I KEEP WONDERING HOW THIS WILL ALL TURN OUT.
I KEEP HAVING A TERRIBLE THOUGHT...
THAT I'LL DIE BEFORE LEARNING.
AND MAYBE I'LL HAVE COST AMELIE HER LIFE, AS WELL.
AND THE THOUGHT HAUNTS ME. THIS...
...IS ALL...MY FAULT.

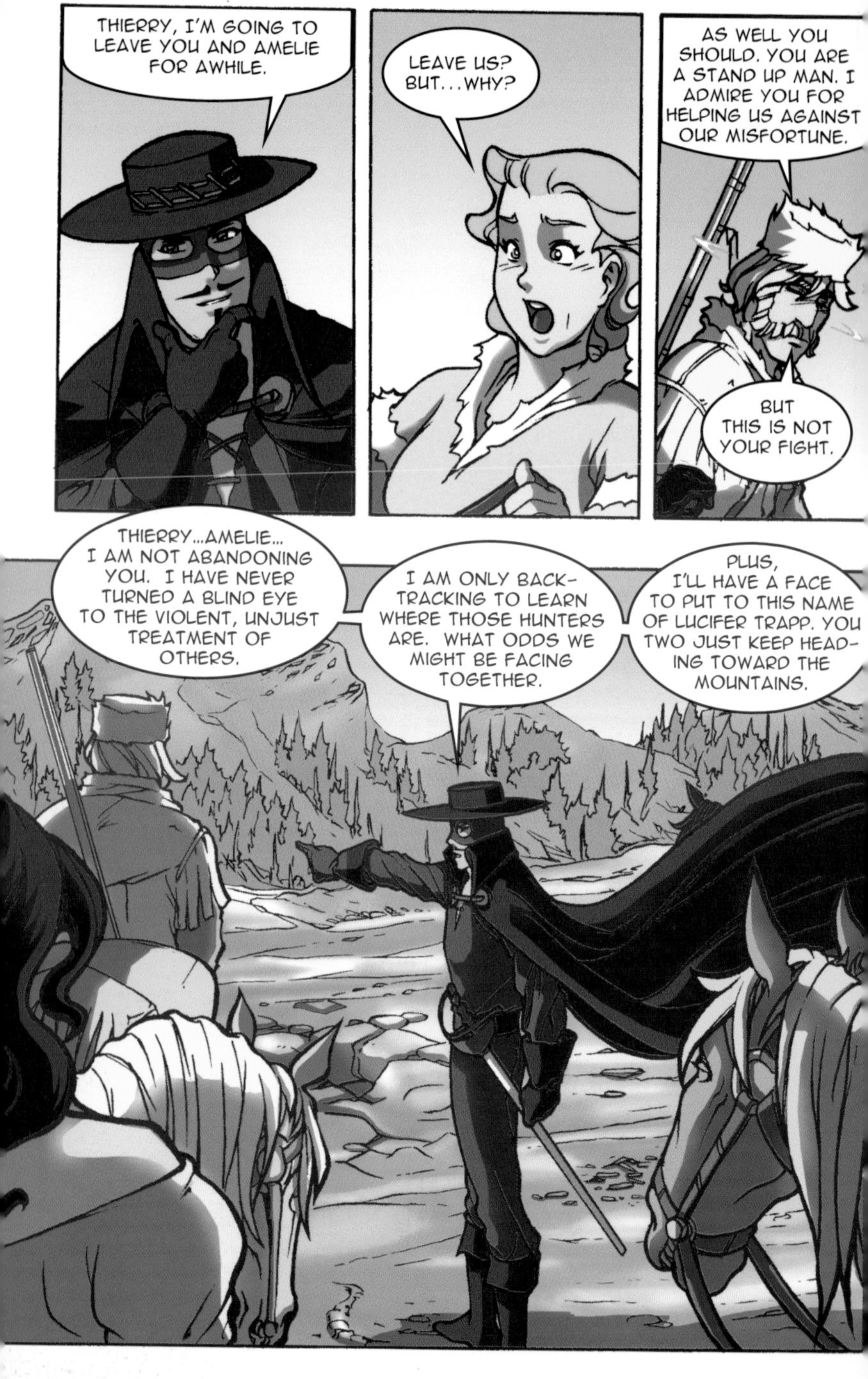
THIERRY, I'M GOING TO LEAVE YOU AND AMELIE FOR AWHILE.
LEAVE US? BUT...WHY?
AS WELL YOU SHOULD. YOU ARE A STAND UP MAN. I ADMIRE YOU FOR HELPING US AGAINST OUR MISFORTUNE.
BUT THIS IS NOT YOUR FIGHT.
THIERRY...AMELIE... I AM NOT ABANDONING YOU. I HAVE NEVER TURNED A BLIND EYE TO THE VIOLENT, UNJUST TREATMENT OF OTHERS.
I AM ONLY BACK-TRACKING TO LEARN WHERE THOSE HUNTERS ARE. WHAT ODDS WE MIGHT BE FACING TOGETHER.
PLUS, I'LL HAVE A FACE TO PUT TO THIS NAME OF LUCIFER TRAPP. YOU TWO JUST KEEP HEAD-ING TOWARD THE MOUNTAINS.

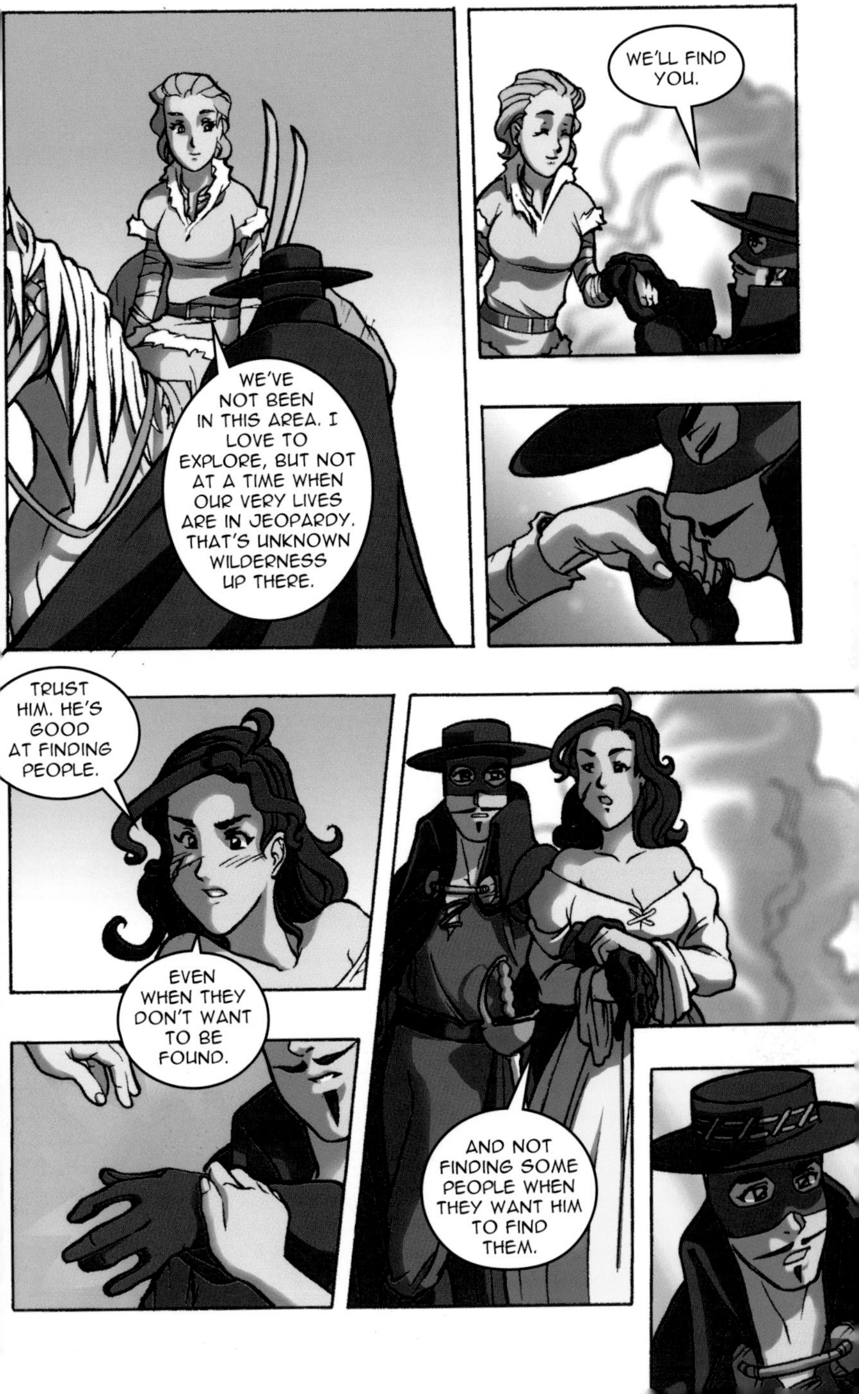
WE'VE NOT BEEN IN THIS AREA. I LOVE TO EXPLORE, BUT NOT AT A TIME WHEN OUR VERY LIVES ARE IN JEOPARDY. THAT'S UNKNOWN WILDERNESS UP THERE.
WE'LL FIND YOU.
TRUST HIM. HE'S GOOD AT FINDING PEOPLE.
EVEN WHEN THEY DON'T WANT TO BE FOUND.
AND NOT FINDING SOME PEOPLE WHEN THEY WANT HIM TO FIND THEM.

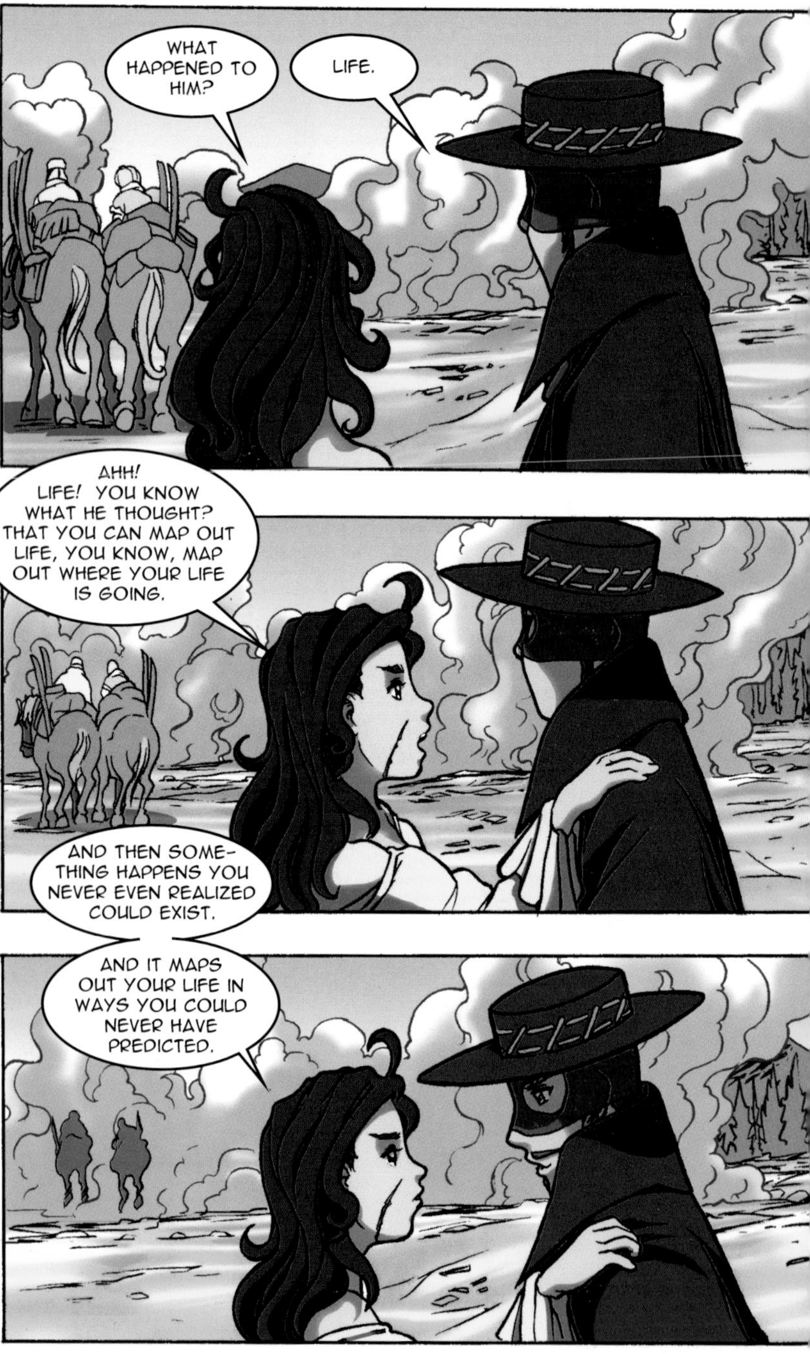

WHAT HAPPENED TO HIM?
LIFE.
AHH! LIFE! YOU KNOW WHAT HE THOUGHT? THAT YOU CAN MAP OUT LIFE, YOU KNOW, MAP OUT WHERE YOUR LIFE IS GOING.
AND THEN SOME-THING HAPPENS YOU NEVER EVEN REALIZED COULD EXIST.
AND IT MAPS OUT YOUR LIFE IN WAYS YOU COULD NEVER HAVE PREDICTED.

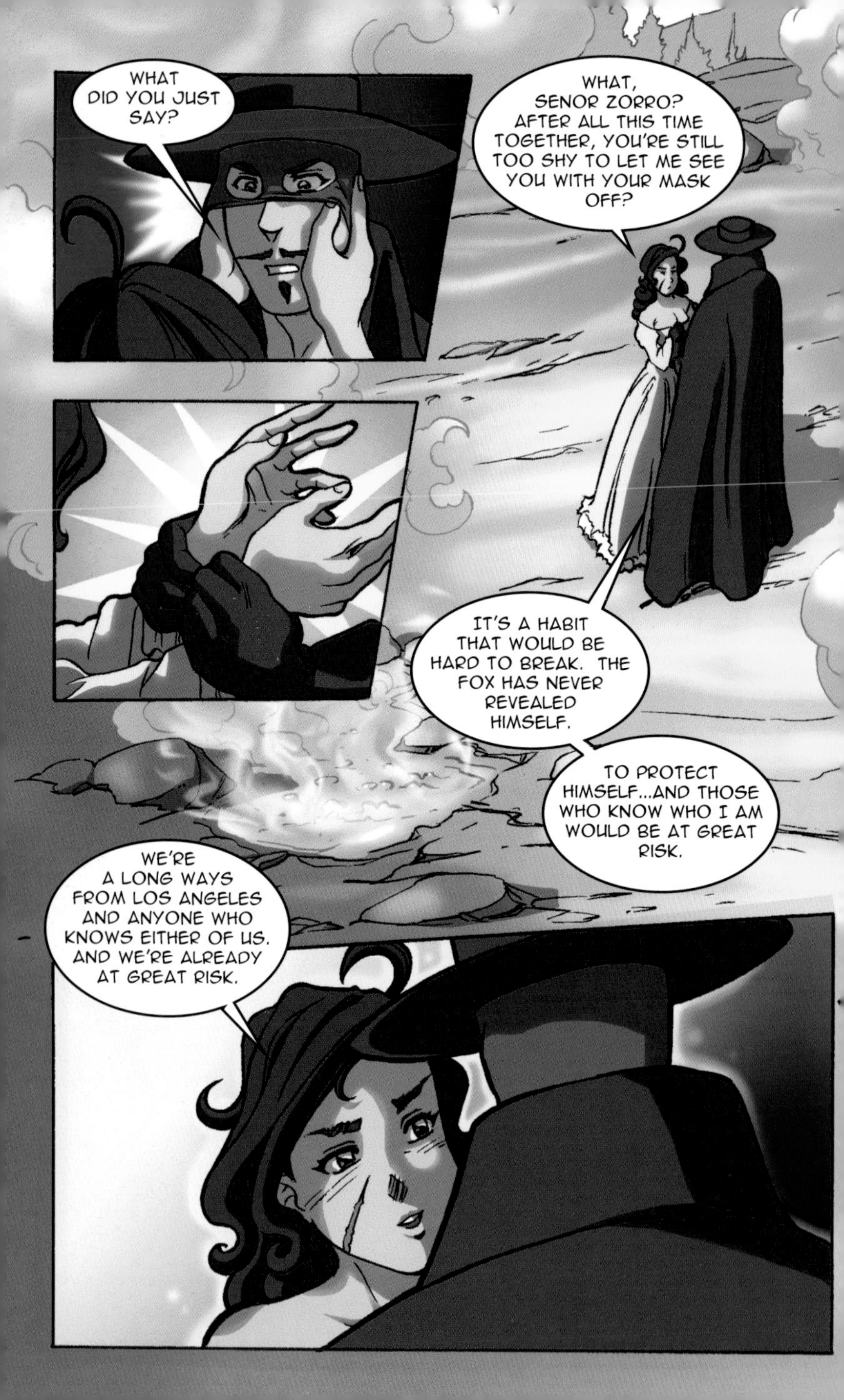
WHAT DID YOU JUST SAY?
WHAT, SENOR ZORRO? AFTER ALL THIS TIME TOGETHER, YOU'RE STILL TOO SHY TO LET ME SEE YOU WITH YOUR MASK OFF?
IT'S A HABIT THAT WOULD BE HARD TO BREAK. THE FOX HAS NEVER REVEALED HIMSELF.
TO PROTECT HIMSELF...AND THOSE WHO KNOW WHO I AM WOULD BE AT GREAT RISK.
WE'RE A LONG WAYS FROM LOS ANGELES AND ANYONE WHO KNOWS EITHER OF US. AND WE'RE ALREADY AT GREAT RISK.

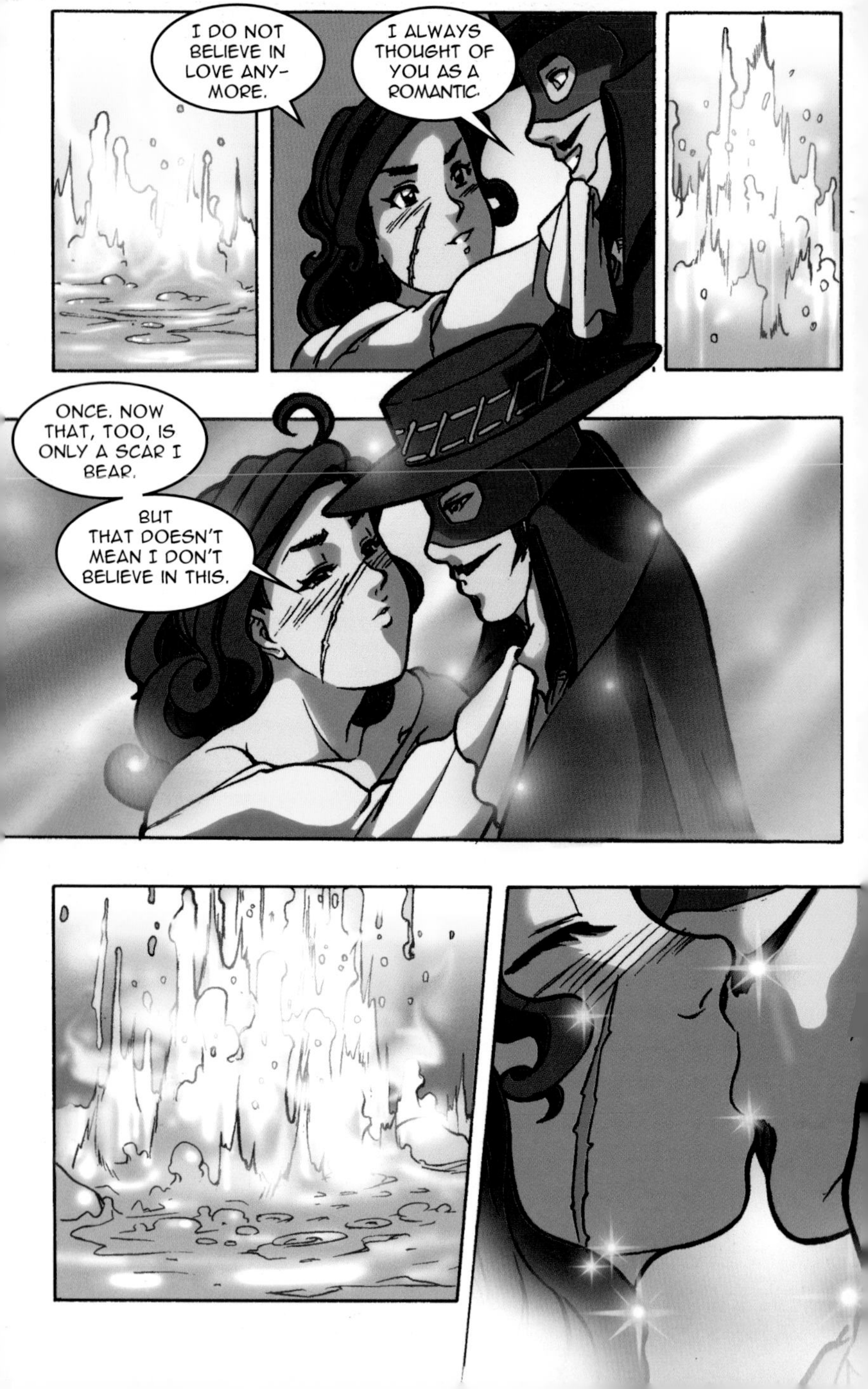
I DO NOT BELIEVE IN LOVE ANY-MORE.
I ALWAYS THOUGHT OF YOU AS A ROMANTIC.
ONCE. NOW THAT, TOO, IS ONLY A SCAR I BEAR.
BUT THAT DOESN'T MEAN I DON'T BELIEVE IN THIS.

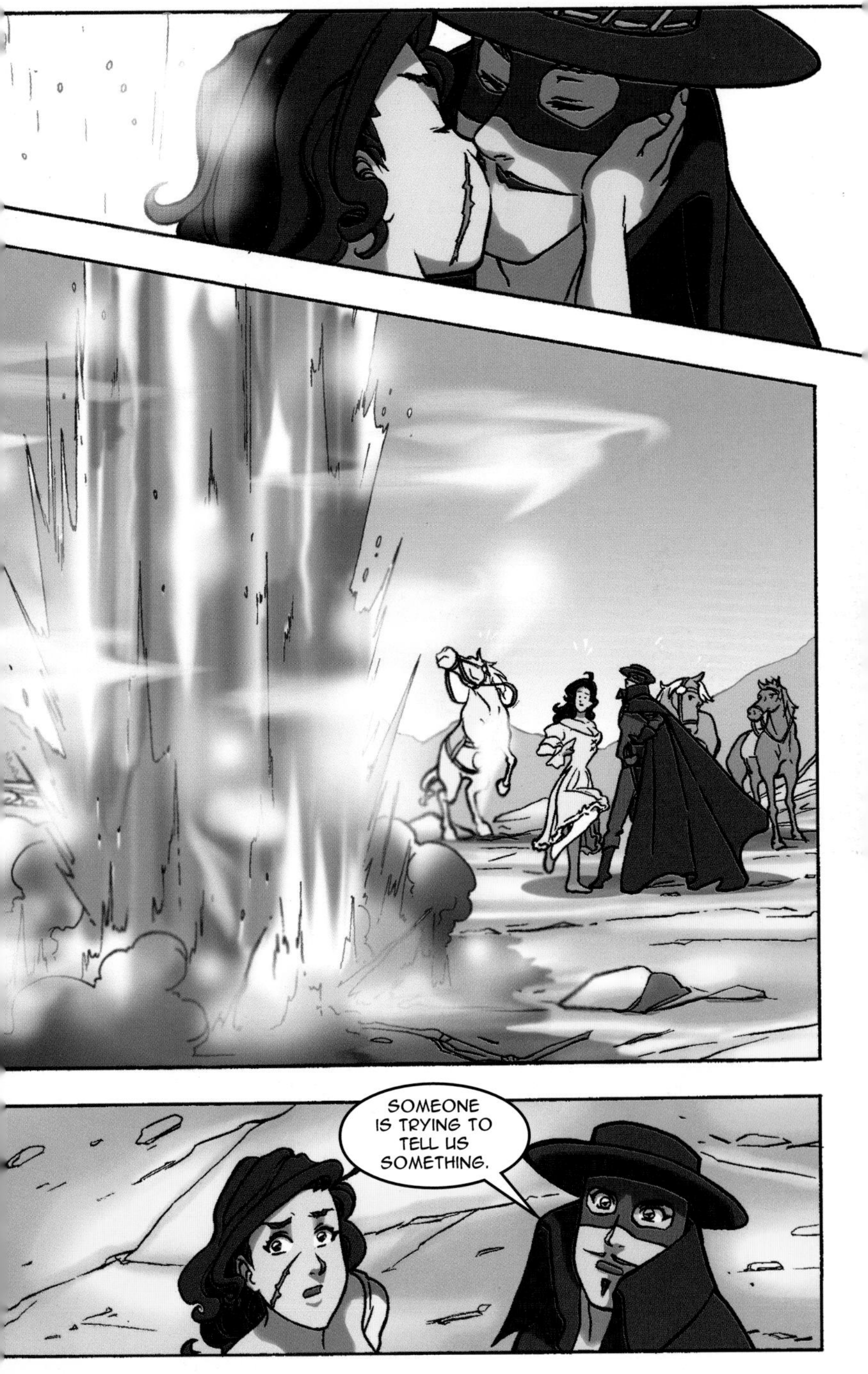
SOMEONE IS TRYING TO TELL US SOMETHING.

WHAT IN THE WORLD IS THAT?

I HAVE NO IDEA WHAT IT IS CALLED.

I'M SURE THE CROW OR THE BLACK FEET OR THE BANNOCKS HAVE NAMES FOR IT.

BUT IT HAS INCREDIBLE FORCE MIXED WITH BEAUTY.

TRULY THE CORRECT TIME TO USE THE WORD "AWESOME" TO DESCRIBE SOMETHING.

AND NOW GONE! POOF! LIKE NATURE HAS PULLED A SPECTACULAR MAGIC TRICK.

LET'S GET OUT OF HERE! I'D ALMOST FEEL SAFER WITH THOSE UGLY HUNTERS.

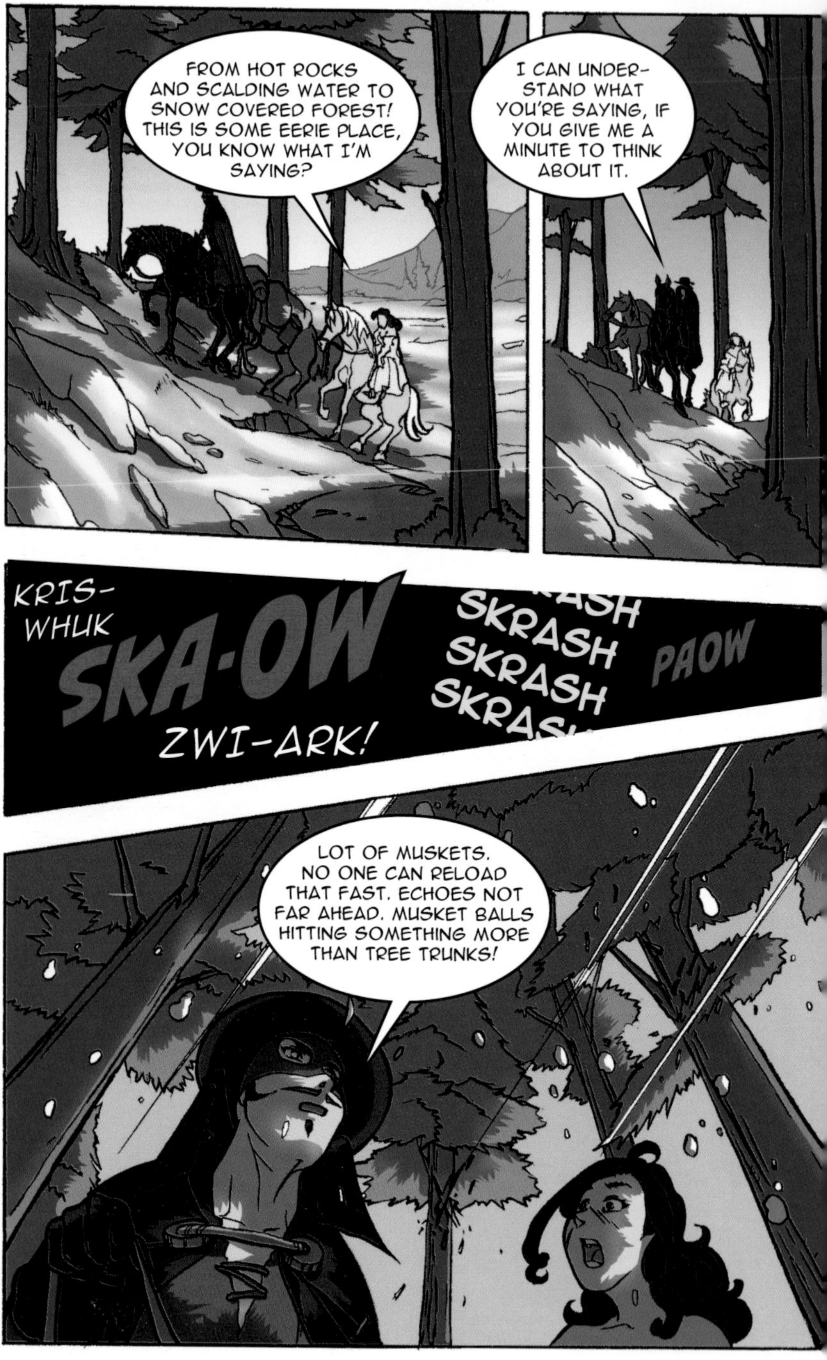
FROM HOT ROCKS AND SCALDING WATER TO SNOW COVERED FOREST! THIS IS SOME EERIE PLACE, YOU KNOW WHAT I'M SAYING?
I CAN UNDER-STAND WHAT YOU'RE SAYING, IF YOU GIVE ME A MINUTE TO THINK ABOUT IT.
KRIS-WHUK
SKA-OW
ZWI-ARK!
SKRASH
SKRASH
SKRASH
PAOW
LOT OF MUSKETS. NO ONE CAN RELOAD THAT FAST. ECHOES NOT FAR AHEAD. MUSKET BALLS HITTING SOMETHING MORE THAN TREE TRUNKS!

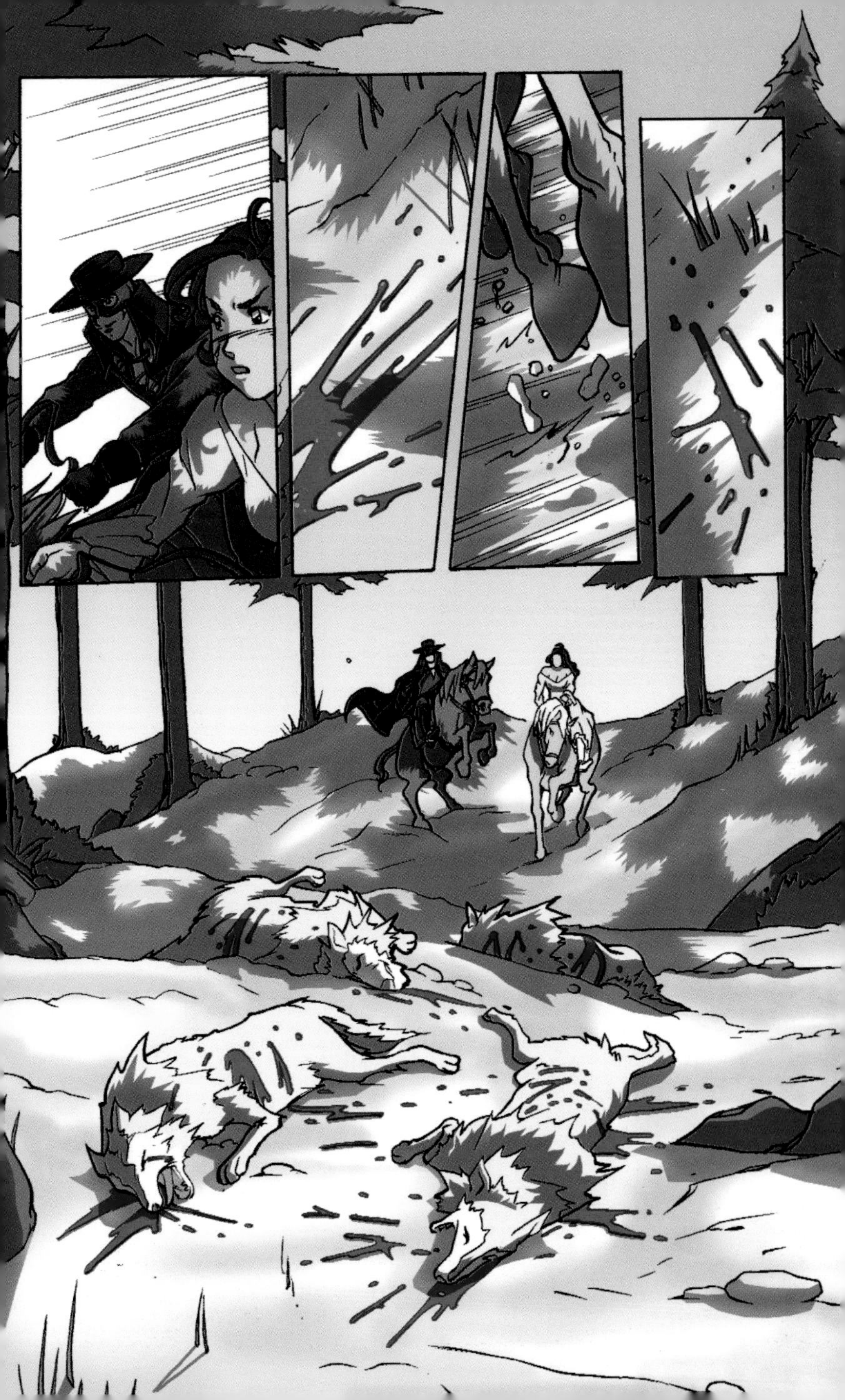

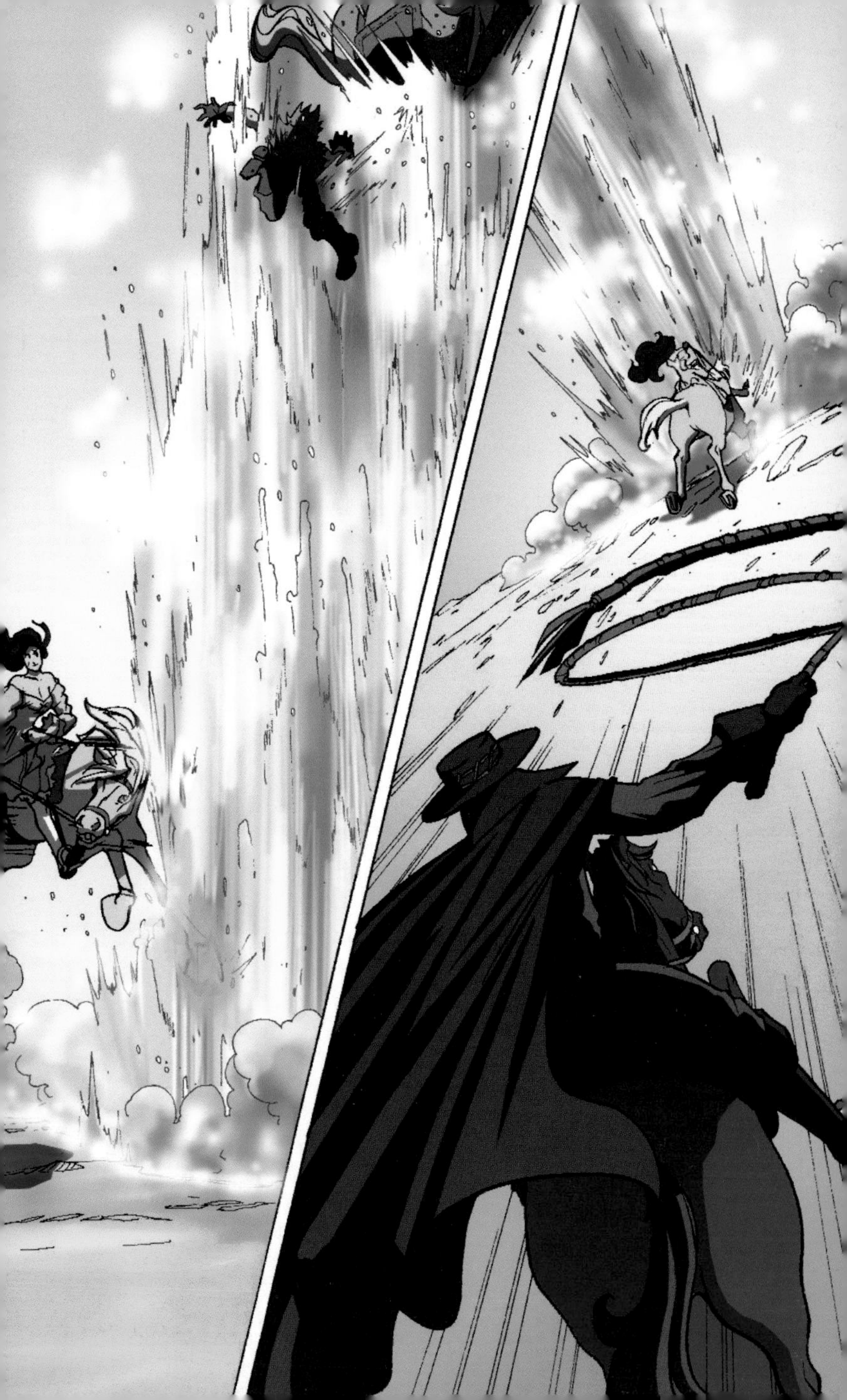

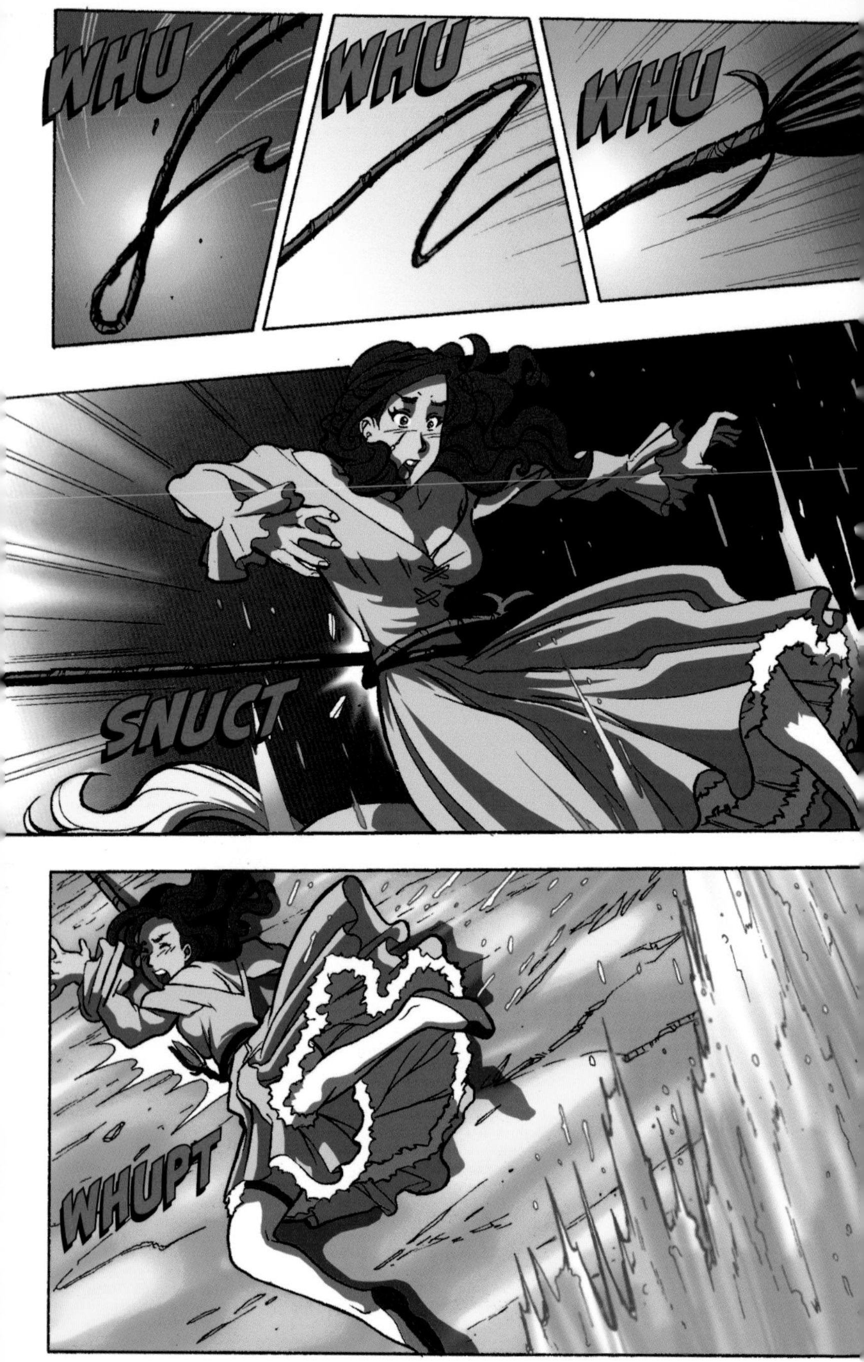
WHU
WHU
WHU
SNUCT
WHUPT

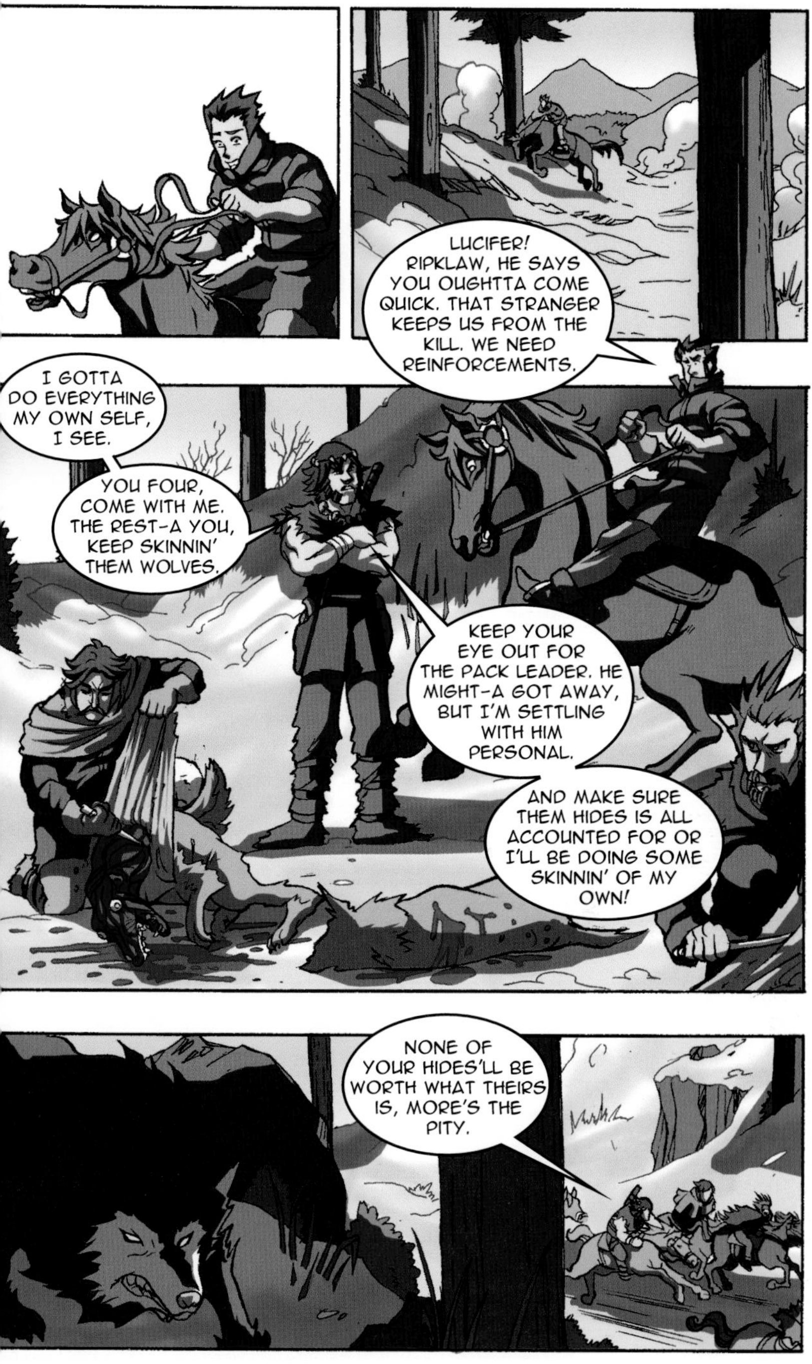
LUCIFER! RIPKLAW, HE SAYS YOU OUGHTTA COME QUICK. THAT STRANGER KEEPS US FROM THE KILL. WE NEED REINFORCEMENTS.
I GOTTA DO EVERYTHING MY OWN SELF, I SEE.
YOU FOUR, COME WITH ME. THE REST-A YOU, KEEP SKINNIN' THEM WOLVES.
KEEP YOUR EYE OUT FOR THE PACK LEADER. HE MIGHT-A GOT AWAY, BUT I'M SETTLING WITH HIM PERSONAL.
AND MAKE SURE THEM HIDES IS ALL ACCOUNTED FOR OR I'LL BE DOING SOME SKINNIN' OF MY OWN!
NONE OF YOUR HIDES'LL BE WORTH WHAT THEIRS IS, MORE'S THE PITY.

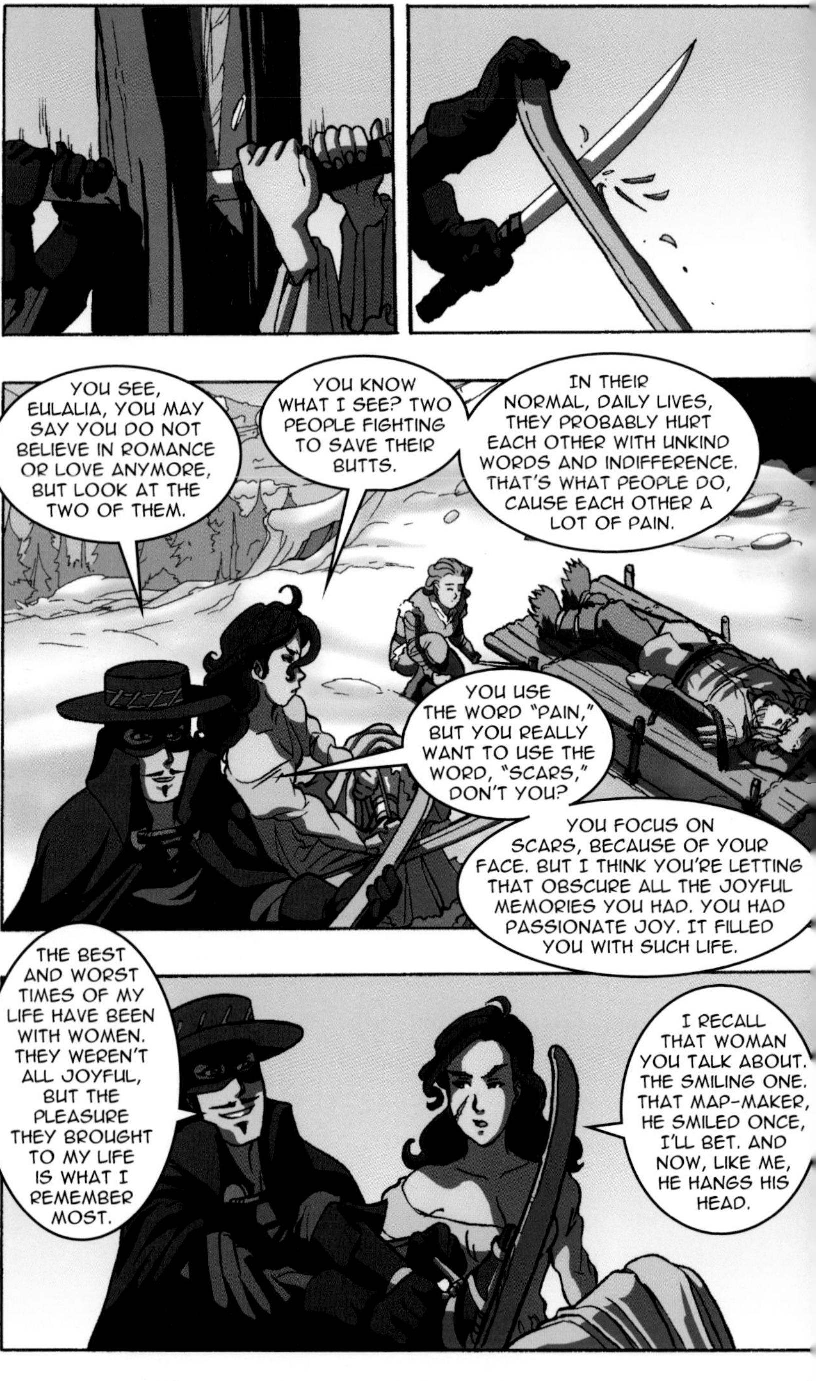

YOU SEE, EULALIA, YOU MAY SAY YOU DO NOT BELIEVE IN ROMANCE OR LOVE ANYMORE, BUT LOOK AT THE TWO OF THEM.
YOU KNOW WHAT I SEE? TWO PEOPLE FIGHTING TO SAVE THEIR BUTTS.
IN THEIR NORMAL, DAILY LIVES, THEY PROBABLY HURT EACH OTHER WITH UNKIND WORDS AND INDIFFERENCE. THAT'S WHAT PEOPLE DO, CAUSE EACH OTHER A LOT OF PAIN.
YOU USE THE WORD "PAIN," BUT YOU REALLY WANT TO USE THE WORD, "SCARS," DON'T YOU?
YOU FOCUS ON SCARS, BECAUSE OF YOUR FACE. BUT I THINK YOU'RE LETTING THAT OBSCURE ALL THE JOYFUL MEMORIES YOU HAD. YOU HAD PASSIONATE JOY. IT FILLED YOU WITH SUCH LIFE.
THE BEST AND WORST TIMES OF MY LIFE HAVE BEEN WITH WOMEN. THEY WEREN'T ALL JOYFUL, BUT THE PLEASURE THEY BROUGHT TO MY LIFE IS WHAT I REMEMBER MOST.
I RECALL THAT WOMAN YOU TALK ABOUT. THE SMILING ONE. THAT MAP-MAKER, HE SMILED ONCE, I'LL BET. AND NOW, LIKE ME, HE HANGS HIS HEAD.

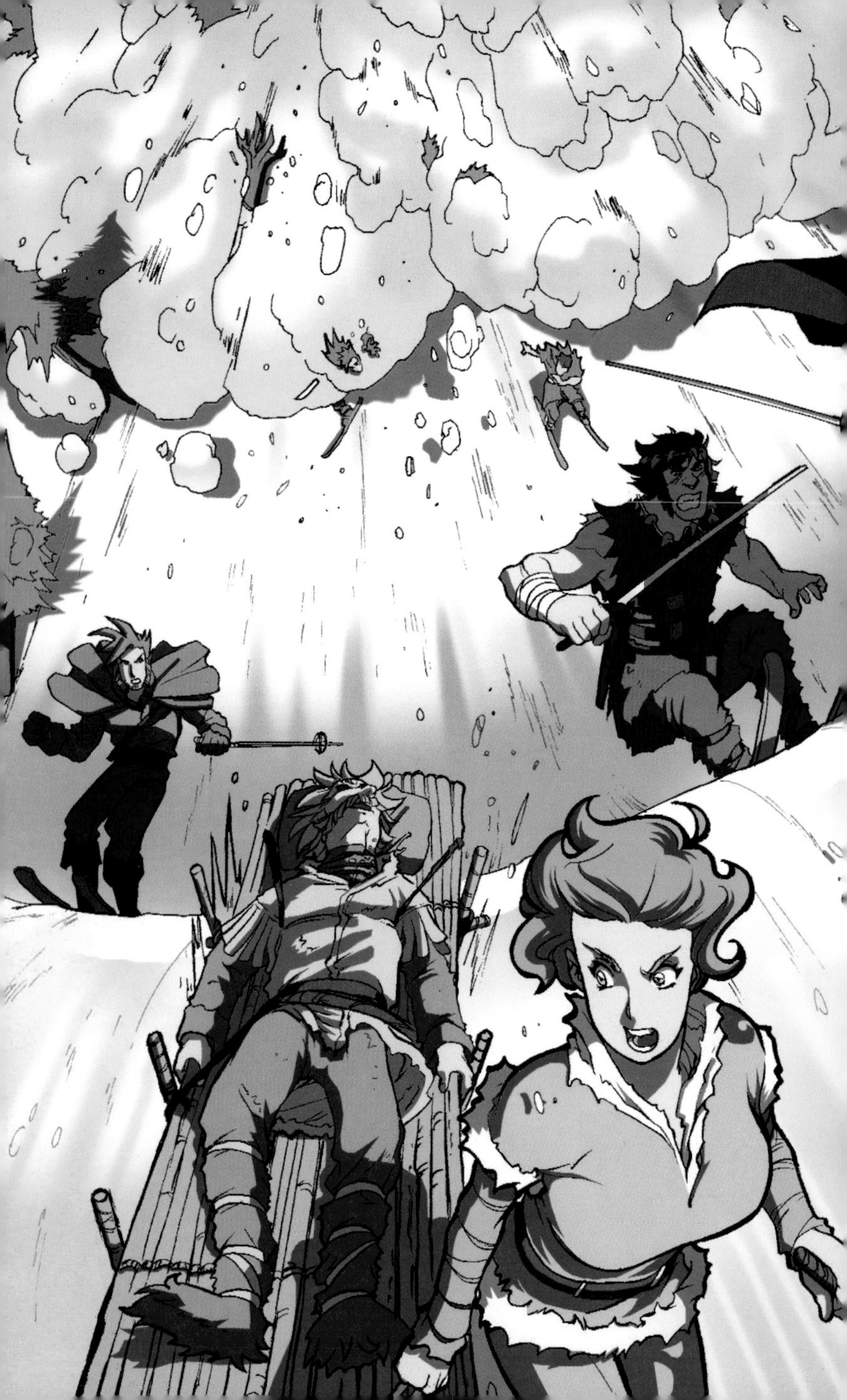

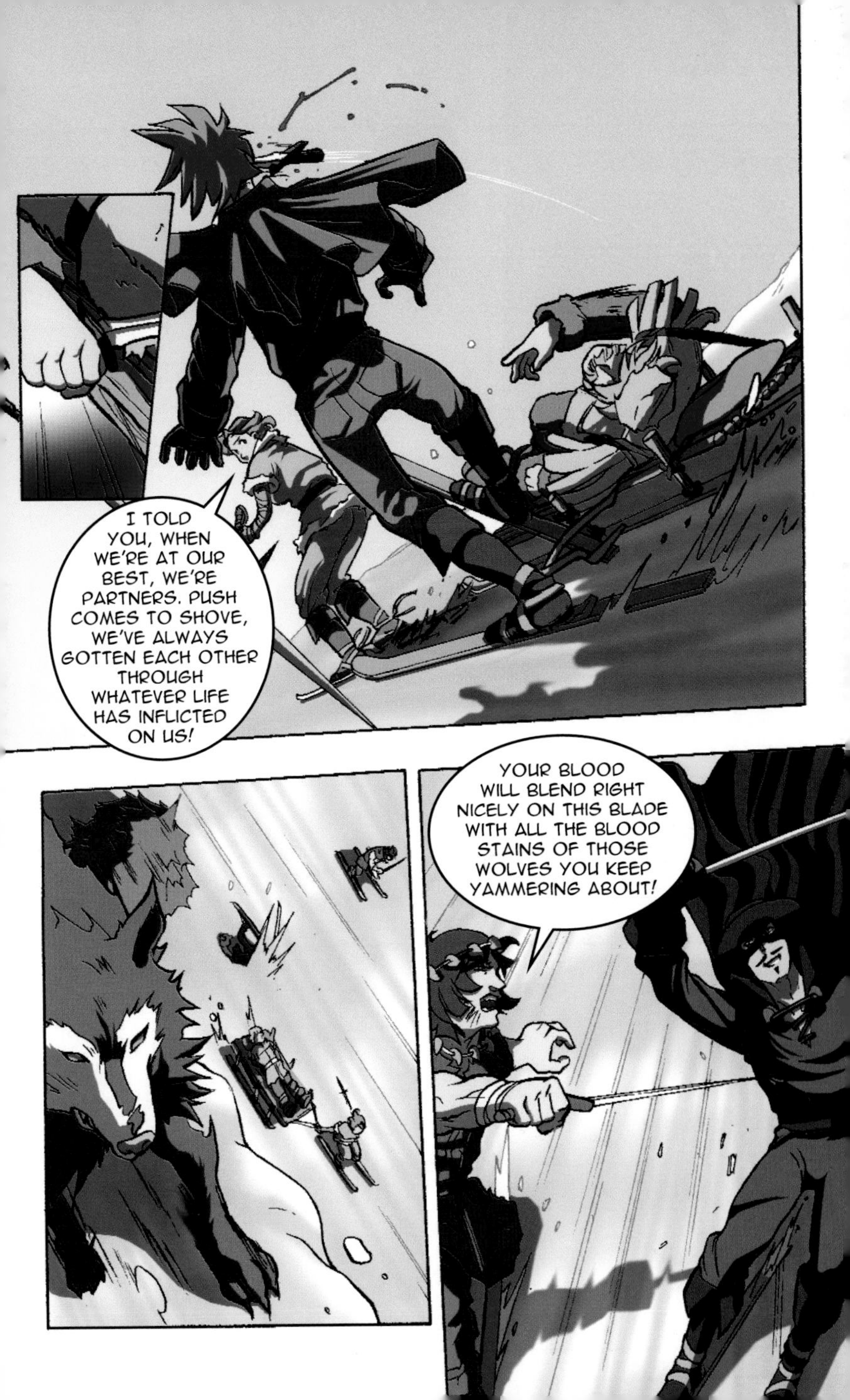
!
I TOLD YOU, WHEN WE'RE AT OUR BEST, WE'RE PARTNERS. PUSH COMES TO SHOVE, WE'VE ALWAYS GOTTEN EACH OTHER THROUGH WHATEVER LIFE HAS INFLICTED ON US!
YOUR BLOOD WILL BLEND RIGHT NICELY ON THIS BLADE WITH ALL THE BLOOD STAINS OF THOSE WOLVES YOU KEEP YAMMERING ABOUT!

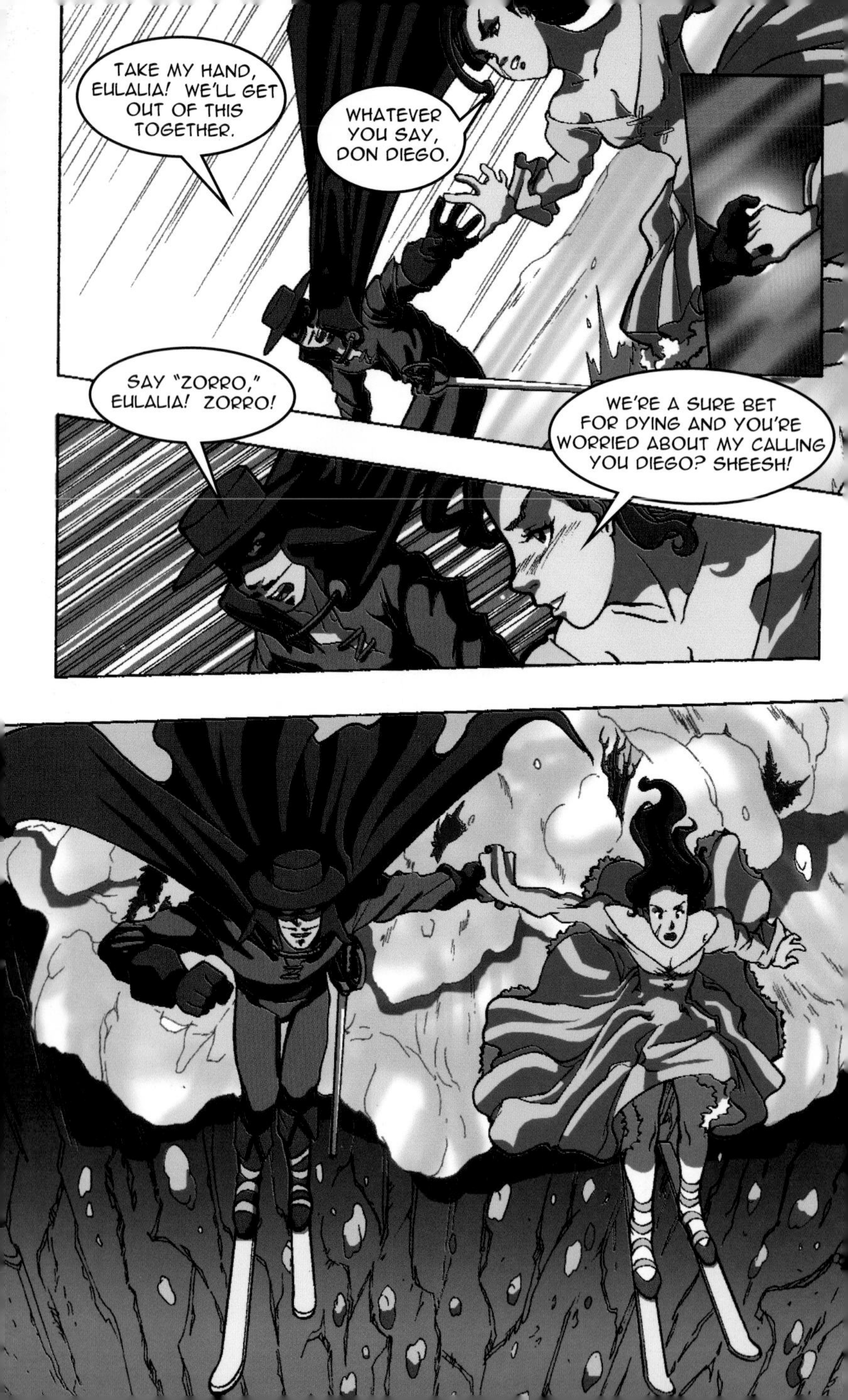
TAKE MY HAND, EULALIA! WE'LL GET OUT OF THIS TOGETHER.
WHATEVER YOU SAY, DON DIEGO.
SAY "ZORRO," EULALIA! ZORRO!
WE'RE A SURE BET FOR DYING AND YOU'RE WORRIED ABOUT MY CALLING YOU DIEGO? SHEESH!

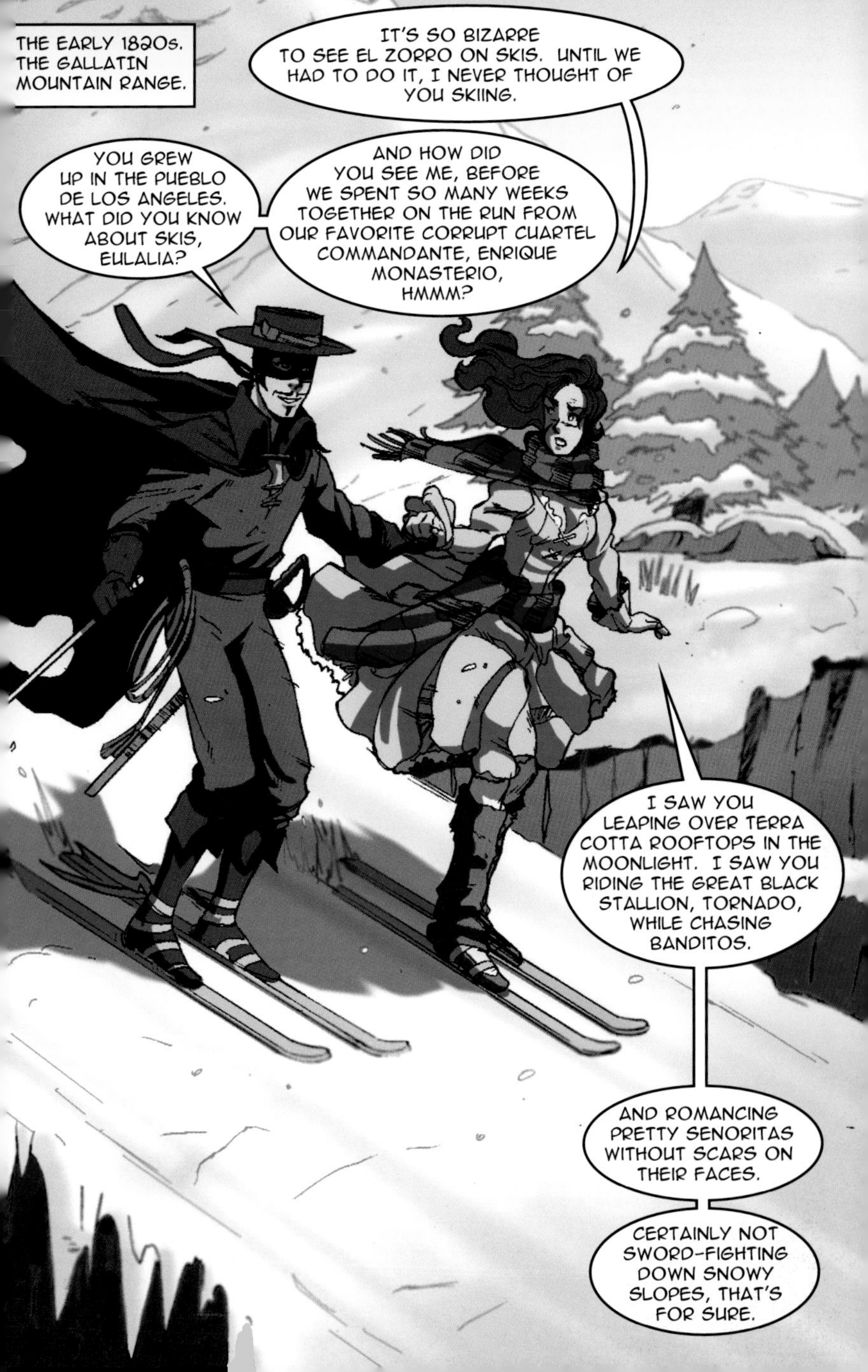
THE EARLY 1820s. THE GALLATIN MOUNTAIN RANGE.
IT'S SO BIZARRE TO SEE EL ZORRO ON SKIS. UNTIL WE HAD TO DO IT, I NEVER THOUGHT OF YOU SKIING.
YOU GREW UP IN THE PUEBLO DE LOS ANGELES. WHAT DID YOU KNOW ABOUT SKIS, EULALIA?
AND HOW DID YOU SEE ME, BEFORE WE SPENT SO MANY WEEKS TOGETHER ON THE RUN FROM OUR FAVORITE CORRUPT CUARTEL COMMANDANTE, ENRIQUE MONASTERIO, HMMM?
I SAW YOU LEAPING OVER TERRA COTTA ROOFTOPS IN THE MOONLIGHT. I SAW YOU RIDING THE GREAT BLACK STALLION, TORNADO, WHILE CHASING BANDITOS.
AND ROMANCING PRETTY SENORITAS WITHOUT SCARS ON THEIR FACES.
CERTAINLY NOT SWORD-FIGHTING DOWN SNOWY SLOPES, THAT'S FOR SURE.

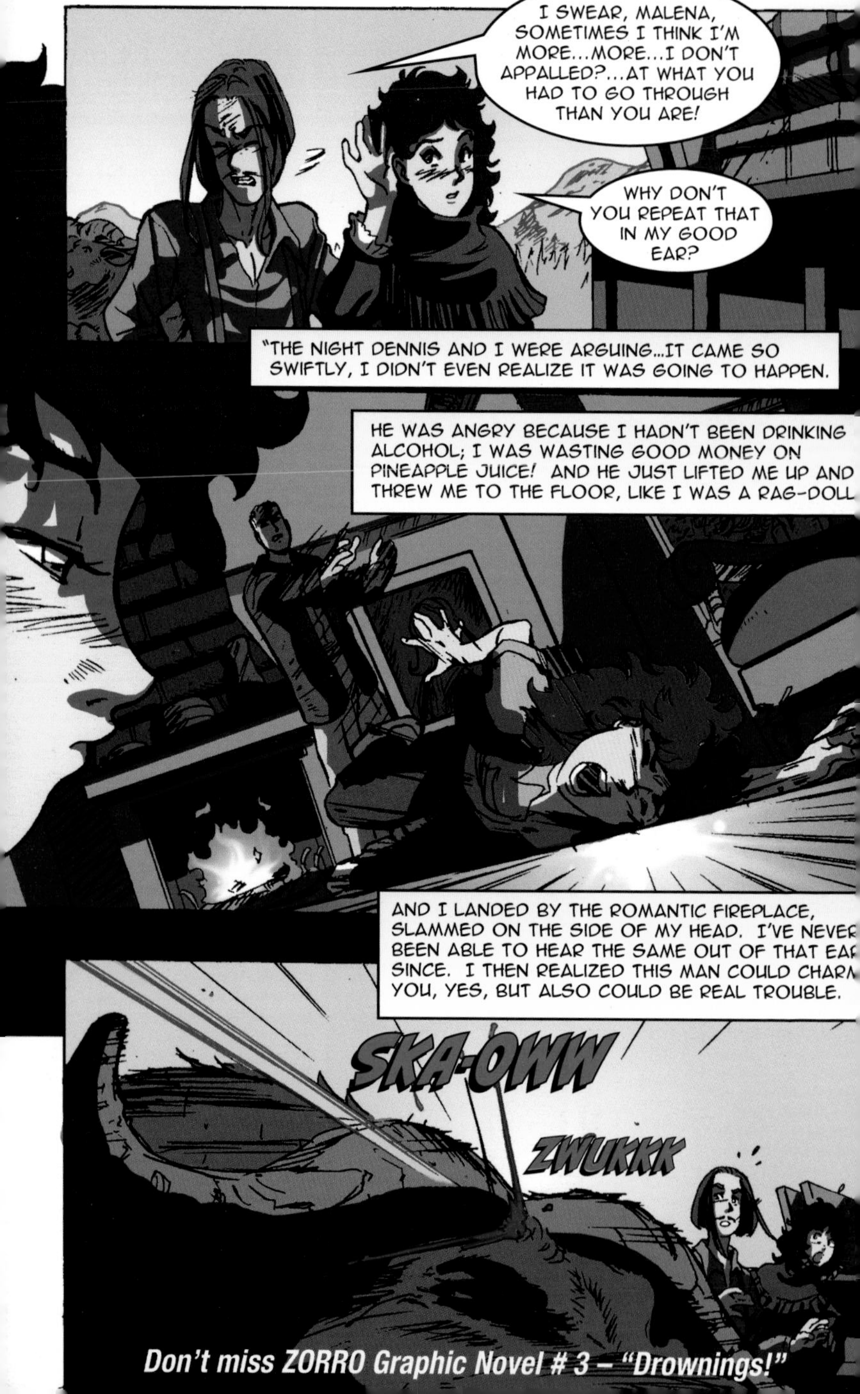
I SWEAR, MALENA, SOMETIMES I THINK I'M MORE...MORE...I DON'T APPALLED?...AT WHAT YOU HAD TO GO THROUGH THAN YOU ARE!
WHY DON'T YOU REPEAT THAT IN MY GOOD EAR?
"THE NIGHT DENNIS AND I WERE ARGUING...IT CAME SO SWIFTLY, I DIDN'T EVEN REALIZE IT WAS GOING TO HAPPEN.
HE WAS ANGRY BECAUSE I HADN'T BEEN DRINKING ALCOHOL; I WAS WASTING GOOD MONEY ON PINEAPPLE JUICE! AND HE JUST LIFTED ME UP AND THREW ME TO THE FLOOR, LIKE I WAS A RAG-DOLL
AND I LANDED BY THE ROMANTIC FIREPLACE, SLAMMED ON THE SIDE OF MY HEAD. I'VE NEVER BEEN ABLE TO HEAR THE SAME OUT OF THAT EAR SINCE. I THEN REALIZED THIS MAN COULD CHARM YOU, YES, BUT ALSO COULD BE REAL TROUBLE.
SKA-OWW
ZWUKKK
Don't miss ZORRO Graphic Novel # 3 – "Drownings!"

The Legend of Zorro

A Novelization By Scott Ciencin
Based on the Screenplay By Roberto Orci
and Alex Kurtzman-Counter

THE LEGEND LIVES ON!

Zorro behind the mask is a daring defender of
freedom and justice, wielding sword and whip
with unparalleled skill in defense of the common
people. Zorro without the mask is Don Alejandro
de la Vega, a wealthy landowner and dedicated
family man.

But ruthless men in a deadly conspiracy of power
have different ideas. As they threaten the future of a
still young state joining the union, they also set
Alejandro's two lives in collision, drawing his beloved
Elena into a perilous world of shadows and lies. Could
the mask ultimately cost the one they call Zorro
everything and everyone he holds most dear? Or will
the Zorro legacy and de la Vega family prevail?

Available in book stores
October 2005
The Legend of Zorro 0-06-083304-1